Praise for *Stella Díaz Never Gives Up*

"Readers don't need familiarity with *Stella Díaz Has Something to Say* to fall in love with [Stella]. The protagonist will endear readers to her; she may also create some environmental converts." —*Kirkus Reviews*

"A stellar sequel or stand-alone title with a plot that strikes the perfect balance between character-driven action and activism."
—*School Library Journal*

Praise for *Stella Díaz Has Something to Say*

2019 Sid Fleischman Award winner
A 2019 ALSC Notable Children's Book
A New York Public Library Best Book for Kids 2018
One of Chicago Public Library's Best of the Best Books 2018

★ "Fans of Clementine and Alvin Ho will be delighted to meet Stella."
—*School Library Journal*, starred review

"Readers should easily relate to Stella, her struggle to use her voice, and the way she feels caught between worlds at school and at home."
—*Publishers Weekly*

"An excellent, empowering addition to middle grade collections." —*Booklist*

"A nice and timely depiction of an immigrant child experience."
—*Kirkus Reviews*

"Readers will a͟ Hill͟ e is, as her
name sugges͟ ͟n's Books

Also by Angela Dominguez

STELLA DÍAZ dreams BIG

¡Mucho!

ANGELA DOMINGUEZ

SQUARE FISH

Roaring Brook Press
New York

SQUARE
FISH

An imprint of Macmillan Publishing Group, LLC
120 Broadway, New York, NY 10271 • mackids.com

Our books may be purchased in bulk for promotional, educational, or
business use. Please contact your local bookseller or the Macmillan Corporate
and Premium Sales Department at (800) 221-7945 ext. 5442 or by email at
MacmillanSpecialMarkets@macmillan.com.

Library of Congress Control Number: 2020912219

Originally published in the United States by Roaring Brook Press
First Square Fish edition, 2022
Book designed by Elizabeth H. Clark
Square Fish logo designed by Filomena Tuosto
Printed in the United States of America by LSC Communications,
Harrisonburg, Virginia.

ISBN 978-1-250-82051-8 (paperback)
3 5 7 9 10 8 6 4 2

Dedicated to my mom, family, and Kyle

Chapter One

"Time for an adventure!" I exclaim.

"Stella? Where are you?" says Nick. I can hear his footsteps coming down the hall.

"I'm in here!" I shout.

"How can you even see in there?" Nick replies, calling to me through the door. "It's so dark."

I step out of the laundry closet wearing a headlamp. Nick quickly looks away from the blinding light.

He groans. "Whoa, what are you doing?"

"I'm getting ready to go camping in the

backyard with Jenny!" I flex my muscles. "It's going to be a real rough-and-tough adventure."

Nick clicks off my headlamp with his thumb and looks me in the eyes. "Stella, I'll believe it when I see it."

"Oh, you'll see," I reply, digging in my fanny pack.

Nick walks away. "Okay. Well, I'm going to be busy with my homework, so you two better stay out of trouble."

Nick has spent most of his Saturday at the kitchen table surrounded by a pile of books. Since Nick started ninth grade, his homework has more than doubled. Almost all his classes have a fat textbook, too. When I tried his backpack on once, I nearly fell backward from the weight of all the books. I want to be just like Nick when I'm in high school, but it's hard to imagine walking around with that backpack. Maybe when I'm his age, I can use two backpacks. That might help.

"You're just jealous you're not invited camping this time," I reply, putting my hands on my hips.

When we were younger, Nick and I would

occasionally camp out in the backyard. Because he's my big brother, he would take care of choosing the perfect spot for our tent and pitching it while I would draw in my sketchbook.

Nick snorts. "Sure. That's it, sis." Then he gets back to doing his homework.

According to my school's calendar, summer is over, but technically there are a few days left till it's autumn. Before we have to start wearing sweaters and parkas, my best friend, Jenny, and I want to make the most of the nice weather, which is why I suggested having a Saturday backyard sleepover. It's going to be so much fun. Sleepovers are already the best, but they're even better when they're outside.

When Jenny arrives, she hands me a glass casserole dish filled with spring rolls her mom made and says, "I have new dance moves to show you."

"Can't wait!" I reply, hugging the casserole. I can't wait for the spring rolls either.

With our arms full of camping equipment, we open the patio doors to go outside. We're hit with a refreshing breeze. It still feels like summer, but there is already an orange leaf or two on our oak tree hinting that fall is coming soon. The backyard is mostly quiet except for the rumble of the Metra, our local train line, in the distance.

I inhale deeply. "It's a perfect night for camping."

Jenny nods and looks at me. "Stella, have you ever been camping? My mom never wants to go. She thinks there will be too many bugs."

I turn *roja* like my red sleeping bag. I may look like an expert, but I've never been camping outside of my backyard in Chicago. Well, never *successfully*. Our family tried to go once in Wisconsin. Mom had seen pictures of a coworker's trip and thought it looked fun. We bought a ton of camping gear for this one trip, packed up our car, and drove out to the campsite. Then we unloaded everything, set up our tent . . . and realized how cold it was! We didn't last a whole night, even with a campfire nearby. We were asleep back in our beds before midnight. Ever since then, the camping gear mostly stays in our laundry closet except for adventures like tonight.

"No, but we're outdoors." I shrug my shoulders and add, "It's probably about the same."

Jenny looks at me wistfully. "I wish we were camping for real. Somewhere amazing, like Montana."

I nod. "But this is still fun! And I'm sure it's only a little bit different."

Jenny smiles and shakes her head as we get to work. She takes the poles out of the tent bag while I lay the tent flat on the ground. Then we snap each pole into place, making sure to get them all through the loops. Like magic, our tent pops up.

"Can I show you some of my new choreography now?" Jenny asks eagerly.

Recently, Jenny joined a new dance class. It meets once a week, but she proudly tells me that it's much harder than her dance summer camp. She's even dancing with the older girls, too!

She stands on our small backyard deck, her makeshift stage, and I sit down on the grass below.

Just as Jenny begins to twirl on her tippy-toes, I spy a shadowy figure peeking out from the patio door.

Nick yells, "Yeah, this is real rugged camping!"

I stick my tongue out at him.

He snickers. "I'll leave you two alone with the elements. Give me a shout when you get hungry."

Then he closes the door.

Jenny ignores him and continues with her performance. For the grand finale, she even leaps! I clap when she bows at the end.

"Brava!" I cheer.

Next we put the finishing touches on our campsite. Once we make our tent cozy with lanterns, pillows, and our spring roll rations, we jump inside and zip the door shut.

"What now? Should we draw?" I ask, scratching my head. I'm not quite sure what people do when they go camping. I start searching my fanny pack for pencils.

Jenny replies, "Well, we could tell ghost stories."

I grab a pillow. "I don't know, Jenny. I don't like scary stories." My shoulders tense up just thinking about it.

"Let's try one. Scary stories are part of the sleepover experience," she says knowingly.

As Jenny begins to tell a story about a dark and stormy night, the wind suddenly picks up. The leaves start to rustle, and the branches creak on the oak tree. The noises from the Metra now sound like ghostly whistles. I quickly realize that we're absolutely alone in the backyard, with only a nylon tent to protect us.

Jenny pauses and turns toward me. She looks nervous. "Did you hear that?"

"What? Did you hear something?" I squeeze my pillow even tighter. I didn't hear anything, but maybe Jenny has super hearing.

We look at each other. Suddenly we hear what sounds like a branch cracking above our heads. Without saying a word, we jump out of the tent and run back inside the house.

As we close the patio door behind us, I turn to Jenny.

"Good thing we're not in Montana."

She nods and locks the door.

Chapter Two

While we are pretty sure there is nothing in the backyard, Jenny and I end up sleeping in the living room, just in case. Nick helps me put *The Undersea World of Jacques Cousteau* on the television so that Jenny and I can fall asleep to Jacques's gentle French accent.

Watching Jacques and his group exploring the oceans is captivating. The whooshing sound of the divers breathing heavily in their scuba masks also makes my eyes heavy.

"I almost forgot!" Jenny says, sitting up in her sleeping bag.

"What?" I ask, yawning. All the commotion must have made me sleepy.

"You're going to love this."

I roll over. "Tell me in the morning."

"My mom registered me for swimming classes at the YMCA."

I pop up. "You're right. I want to join!"

On the first day of fourth grade, I made a list of dreams for the school year. Big dreams, like win an award, work on a big project, and make new types of art, just to name a few. I even wrote *Nobel Prize*, but I had to cross it out. Turns out they don't have one just for kids. While swim lessons might not be on my official list, swimming does sound fun. I guess I'll just have to add it to the list.

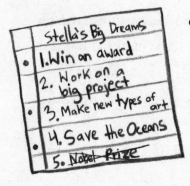

"Yes! I bet my mom could drive you, too. It's only on Wednesdays, and the session starts in two weeks," Jenny says.

I nod. "I'll ask my mom when she gets home."

I look at the clock on

the TV stand. It's almost 10:00 P.M., and Mom's still not home yet. She is at her first-ever "Girls' Night" with her coworkers at the radio station. Now that Nick is fifteen and can officially babysit me alone, Mom is beginning to hang out with work friends a bit more. I'm happy for her, but it's awfully late, and I want to ask her about the swim lessons right now. Plus, I can't really fall asleep until Mom tucks me in and says, "*Te quiero, mi estrellita.*"

To which I always reply, "I love you, too, Mom."

I try to stay awake so I can see her when she gets home, but Jacques Cousteau's voice is too soothing. I fall fast asleep and dream of swimming in the deep blue sea.

In the morning, I wake up to the smell of batter and the sound of Mom humming. Jenny and I head to the kitchen to investigate.

"*Buenos días.* How did the sleepover go, *niñas*?" Mom says, flipping a pancake over. "I noticed that you two decided not to sleep outside."

We start giggling just thinking about our

adventure last night. The only way I can sum it up is to say, "Camping was an experience."

"*Muy interesante.*" She laughs. "You'll have to tell me more about it later."

Mom hands us plates, and we serve ourselves breakfast. Jenny devours her pancakes with lakes of maple syrup on top.

"I never get to eat this at home," Jenny says in between bites. "Our pancakes are way different."

She pours more maple syrup onto her plate.

Jenny's mom makes pancakes, but they are Vietnamese-style. Their pancakes are made out of rice flour and filled with meat or veggies. I've had them at her house, and they're yummy, but they are definitely not syrupy sweet like this.

When Jenny's mom arrives to pick her up, Jenny whispers to me at the front door, "Don't forget to ask your mom about swim lessons."

"I'm on it," I reply, giving her a high five.

I help Mom clean up in the kitchen. She leaves out one plate of pancakes, ready for when Nick finally wakes up. She even put chocolate chips in his batch because those are his favorites.

"How was Girls' Night?" I ask. Then I lean in closer and make my voice stern. "And when exactly did you get home, young lady?"

"*Perdonéme, jefa*," she teases, calling me her boss. "Ten forty-two in the evening. I gave you a kiss on the cheek, but you were wiped out."

"Oh," I reply. That's not so late. Camping must have really made me tired!

She continues, "And Girls' Night was so much fun! I haven't been salsa dancing like that in a long time!"

She busts out into a salsa move in the middle of the kitchen. It's like her feet and hips are twisting with joy.

I frown. Mom and I salsa together all the time. Every Friday we have what she likes to call our "weekly appointment." That's our Friday night tradition where Nick, Mom, and I play games and have family fun time. And Mom and I always end up salsa dancing all around the living room.

Mom sees my face and knows I'm upset.

"*Mi amor*, I misspoke. I know that you and I salsa, but it's different with a live band. *El ritmo* just takes over."

The rhythm must be taking her over now, too, because she cha-chas again.

I nod. I sort of understand. I also know that when we're salsa dancing, Mom slows down for me. I remember when Mom and Dad used to salsa together. Her feet would move at triple the speed. I could never understand how she did it. Suddenly this conversation gives me an idea.

"Mom," I say in my sweetest voice, "speaking of physical activities . . ."

"Sí, Stellita."

"Jenny signed up to take swimming lessons at the YMCA."

"Oh, fun!" she says, wiping down the kitchen counter.

I lean over to get closer to her.

"I was thinking . . . Could I sign up for lessons, too? Jenny said her mom could probably drive me there."

"I don't see why not. Let me double-check with her mom, but it would be good for you. Nick has his karate, after all. It's time you have a sport for yourself, too."

I squeal. That was much easier than I thought it would be! I thought I'd have to tell her that swimming was necessary to my development as a future marine biologist. That it will make me strong just like it did for Jacques Cousteau. Before he became a famous oceanographer, Jacques Cousteau was a sickly kid, and he actually built up his strength by swimming. He grew so strong that he served in the navy and eventually explored all over the world, even Antarctica! I'm a little disappointed I didn't get to share that fact, but there are more important things to think about—like which swimsuit to wear for my first class!

Chapter Three

An hour later, while I'm watching my favorite morning cartoons and Mom scribbles in her day planner, Nick comes downstairs from his room. He has a blanket wrapped around him and heads toward the pancakes without saying a word to us.

"*Hola, niño.*" Mom hands him a plate. Nick smiles sleepily in return.

"Okay, *ahora que estamos juntos,*" Mom begins, commenting that we're all together, "what's on the agenda this Sunday?"

Nick and I look at each other. We both know what the answer is: "Homework."

He adds, "And I've got a shift at the pizzeria this afternoon."

Even though I don't have as much homework as Nick, I do have more homework than I had in third grade. Last year, I'd maybe have a big project or two that we had to work on for a few weeks, like the presentation I did on marine biology. I was so nervous, but I ended up getting an A! But this year, we have homework almost every night, even on the weekends. This weekend, I have to complete a worksheet on long division and write a poem about my favorite subject. Other kids might complain about having more homework, but I like it. It makes me feel grown up like Mom and Nick.

Mom asks, "Do either of you need my help with homework?"

"Maybe?" I reply, while Nick shakes his head.

Mom says, "Let's go over your homework now, Stella, and see if anything is tricky."

I nod excitedly. I love it when Mom has the time to help me.

"Then I'll run some errands," she says as she reviews her day planner. "It's going to be a busy week at the radio station. We're getting ready for the big Mexican Independence Day festival and the rest of the fall events, like Día de los Muertos."

Mom looks at her hands. "Hopefully, I can get my nails done today, too."

Even though Mom is busy, she always tries to have "me time" at the nail salon. She says that the right nail color brings her good luck.

I move from the kitchen counter to get my backpack when suddenly there is a knock at the front door.

"Are you expecting anyone?" Mom asks, looking at us.

Nick and I shake our heads.

"Maybe Jenny left something behind," she says.

Nick says, "Or maybe it's Linda."

I clap my hands together. "And Biscuit!"

I look forward to any opportunity to see our neighbor Linda and her adorable Chihuahua.

Mom walks to the door, and I follow her like a puppy. But to our surprise, it's not Linda. It's quite the opposite of Linda. Instead of an older woman, it's a man around Mom's age. He's wearing a Cubs baseball cap, and he looks a little sweaty.

"Hello. How can I help you?" Mom asks in her deep, serious voice, the one she uses whenever she is trying to sound fierce.

He waves his hand to say hello. "I'm sorry to bother you. I'm your new neighbor. I just moved into the apartment across the street."

He points at the brick house with the blue door and petunias in its flower boxes. When I look over, I notice the FOR RENT sign that was on the lawn is now gone.

"Oh, hi," Mom replies. Her right eyebrow is still cautiously raised.

He continues, "I've got my moving van temporarily double-parked. I am just checking with the neighbors that I'm not blocking anyone in."

I notice he has an accent like Mom's. I wonder if he speaks Spanish, too.

"It's no problem," Mom says, smiling. "Thanks for checking!"

"I really appreciate it." He sighs. "It should be only an hour at most. It's just me and my daughter, Izzy. We don't have a ton of stuff."

"Daughter?" I say without thinking.

He smiles. "Yup! She's a little older than you, I think."

"Izzy is a cute name." Mom extends her hand. "I'm Perla, by the way."

"Diego," he replies, shaking her hand. "*¡Mucho gusto!*"

I smile at Mom. He does, indeed, speak Spanish! I wonder if he is from Mexico like us. While I barely remember Mexico because we moved to Chicago when I was a baby, Mom grew up there and has never lost her accent. Though I never notice Mom's accent until strangers point it out. She just sounds like Mom to me.

"*Igualmente*, Diego. If you need anything, let us know!"

"Welcome to the neighborhood!" I add. I turn a little *roja* when I say it. I'm still kind of shy around new people.

"*¡Gracias!* I better run," says Diego. Walking away, he adds, "*¡Adiós!*"

"*Hasta pronto*," Mom replies with a wave.

Mom closes the door and looks at me.

"Well, he seems like he'll be a nice addition to the neighborhood," she says.

I nod. He may be a stranger, but he does have a daughter. Maybe Izzy and I can be friends! Better yet— maybe she'll want to be a Sea Musketeer, too! The Sea Musketeers is a club I started with some of the kids who attended summer camp with me at the Shedd Aquarium. And my school friends Jenny and Stanley joined, too. Our mission: to help protect the oceans. We could always use more members in the crusade!

"We should make them some food tonight once we're done with all our chores and errands," Mom says. "It'll be neighborly. Plus, it will be a relaxing activity before the busy week."

"You should make a *quesadilla*, but the one *mi abuela* makes, not the tortilla one," I suggest, licking my lips as I think about the cheesy sweet bread from El Salvador. It's very different from the Mexican kind but just as *delicioso*. I add, "And I can be the official taste tester."

"Deal, but only after you put the camping gear back in the closet," Mom replies, looking outside at the backyard.

I turn *roja* again. I had forgotten the worst part of camping is packing everything up. I nod, and then we shake hands to seal the deal.

Chapter Four

The next morning before school, Mom and I quietly drop off the *quesadilla* on Diego's doorstep. It's still early, so we don't want to knock on the door, just in case he is sleeping. We wrapped it safely in a glass food container and included a note welcoming him to the neighborhood signed by the three of us. Nick didn't want to sign the note at first, until I told him Diego was wearing a Cubs baseball cap.

As we head back to the car, I turn to see Diego open the front door and grab the treat from his doorstep. He's dressed in his work clothes. Once he reads the note, he waves to us.

"*¡Muchas gracias!*" he thanks us.

"*¡De nada!*" I shout *you're welcome* from the car door.

On the way to school, Mom blasts salsa music, smiling and even shimmying to the beat. It's only me and her in the car now that Nick is in high school. He gets a ride with his friend Jason since his school starts earlier than mine.

Mom plants a giant kiss on my cheek when we arrive at my school, Arlington Heights Elementary.

"*Que tengas un buen día, mi estrella,*" she says, telling me to have a great day.

I wipe the lipstick from my cheek. "You have the bestest day, *Mamá,*" I reply.

As I walk up to the school, I can feel itty-bitty butterflies fluttering in my stomach. I've always liked school, but it can be hard, too. Sometimes I feel like I stick out when all I want to do is hide like a hermit crab.

But now that I'm in fourth grade, I don't feel quite as shy as I used to. That might be because I have class with my friends, but I think the real reason is that I have the best teacher this year.

"*Hola*, Ms. Benedetto," I say when I enter the classroom. I hand her my completed homework.

Ms. Benedetto greets everyone with a warm smile, but she makes you feel like she's only smiling for you.

"*Buenos días*, Stella," she replies, looking up from her laptop.

Ms. Benedetto likes it when I speak Spanish. She even studied abroad in Spain during college. She says knowing two languages makes you smarter. It's a relief to know that if I were to slip up and say a word in Spanish instead of English, she wouldn't be upset with me.

For that reason and many more, Ms. Benedetto might be my all-time favorite teacher, or at least tied with Ms. Bell, my third-grade teacher.

"Howdy!" says Stanley, pulling out his chair. He sits next to me at our table of four. According to Stanley, everyone in Texas says *howdy* instead of *hello*, and even though he's lived in Chicago for over a year now, he still greets people like a Texan. That's one thing that makes Stanley a fun friend. He is never boring, because he has his own way of doing things.

"Did you finish your homework?" I ask, settling in at my desk.

Stanley nods. "I wrote my poem on outer space." Stanley is as obsessed with space as I am with the oceans. In fact, today he's wearing a new T-shirt with a picture of the solar system on it. He even went to NASA summer camp, where he became a junior explorer.

"I wrote mine on the oceans," I reply.

I hear a guffaw.

"Could you be more predictable?" Ben Shaw says.

Ben is one of our other tablemates. Ben was in our class last year and knows about my ocean obsession. Ben has also been the class clown as long as I have known him, but this year, he is less funny and just plain mean. Like when Anna tripped over her shoelaces last week, he called her a klutz all day long.

"Haha, good one, Ben," says Jeremy in between chuckles.

Jeremy is Ben's friend and sits beside him at our

table. He's much quieter than Ben. That is, until Ben makes a joke. Then he falls over laughing and occasionally snorting.

Stanley and I roll our eyes.

The rest of the class trickles in before the bell rings. Jenny waves at me from the table next to mine. She's seated next to her friend Anna and Anna's best friend, Isabel. Chris Pollard makes up the fourth at their table. Chris used to hang out with Ben last year, but it seems like something's changed between them.

Although Jenny and I might not be at the same table, it makes me happy to have Jenny back in my class again. I missed her a lot when we were in different classes last year. Now all I have to do is turn my head, and I can wave at my best friend. I also don't have to worry about finding her at lunch, because we just walk to the cafeteria together. That's simply amazing.

After the bell rings, Ms. Benedetto walks out in front of the class to go over the agenda. I notice she's wearing her favorite pattern—animal print!—on her feet. Her shoes are zebra-print ballet flats. Ms. Benedetto loves animals. She's even a vegetarian because she doesn't want to harm a single one.

"Class, now that we're a bit more adjusted to being back at school and all the permission slips are signed, we're going to start an exciting way to learn science for the rest of the year. We'll be doing weekly labs."

I sit up tall and whisper to myself, "Yes, finally!"

Labs are definitely on my list of dreams for fourth grade. It fits nicely in the "big projects" section. Now if I can only get a ribbon or trophy for the labs, that would check a second item off my list.

She continues, "The idea is, we will work on projects or experiments built by your hands. Sometimes you might even need to problem solve to come up with unique solutions!"

Stanley and I look at each other.

"This is just like my summer camp," he whispers as I nod in agreement.

We both made our own exciting projects at our camps over the summer. I made an enrichment toy for a dolphin to play with at the Shedd Aquarium summer camp, while Stanley made a robot at his NASA camp.

Ms. Benedetto explains, "For starters, I want you to select a partner at your table. This will be your partner till the end of the first six weeks."

Without hesitation, Stanley and I decide to work together, while Ben and Jeremy pair up.

"Our first project is an edible project. We'll be learning about plants and geology through creating a soil model," says Ms. Benedetto.

"Ugh, does this mean we're going to eat real soil?" Isabel asks.

Anna says, "My dog, Scout, eats soil. I don't think it looks delicious."

Ms. Benedetto laughs. "You'll just have to wait and see."

As Ms. Benedetto demonstrates the different levels

of soil on the whiteboard, we take careful notes. Then Ms. Benedetto drops off all the materials at each table, including rubber gloves.

"Scientists must keep their stations free of contamination," she remarks.

As I put on my gloves, I squirm just imagining what gross things I might have to touch.

"You all may begin," Ms. Benedetto says when she gets back to the front of the classroom. Then she adds, "Watch out for the red buckets. They have worms in them."

I take a deep breath and peek inside the red bucket on the table between me and Stanley. I let out a sigh of relief when I see *gummy worms*, not real ones!

Stanley picks up the bucket. He asks, "Stella, would you ever eat a worm?"

"Maybe," I reply, staring at my red-and-green gummy worm. Then I add, "The grasshoppers I had in Mexico were surprisingly delicious."

I'm not lying either! The grasshoppers we had were

called *chapulines*. We ate them with tortillas and avocado.

"Hmmm . . . I guess I'd give it a shot, then," Stanley says, and then sticks a gummy worm into his mouth. He jiggles it with his fingers before he chomps down on it. Then he grins wide.

"Ew . . . ," I say, grimacing. "Not a live one, though."

"No eating your materials until I say so," announces Ms. Benedetto.

"Sorry!" Stanley replies.

Then we both burst into a giggle.

Ben rolls his eyes at us. "You guys are weird."

"Why do you say that?" I demand. I can feel myself turning a little *roja* with anger, but Stanley shrugs it off. He is like a water-skipper bug. He lets rude comments glide beneath him like water.

"Weird is fun." Stanley crosses his eyes and sticks out his tongue. Then he nudges me. "Right, Stella?"

I nod, feeling much better. I try making the same face, but I can't. I just keep laughing too much at Stanley's silly expression.

Ms. Benedetto looks over at us and motions for us to be quiet. I mouth "Sorry" to her and zip my mouth shut.

"Whatever," Ben mutters with a devious, sharklike smile.

The way Ben is acting is making me nervous, but I can't pinpoint why. I even catch him whispering to Jeremy while looking at us. Fortunately, we have our project to worry about. We silently continue working on our individual soil models from the bottom up. We use chocolate morsels for the bedrock, chocolate pudding for the subsoil, chocolate wafers for the soil, and green-dyed coconut for the grass. Finally, we each place a gummy worm on top of our little jars.

By the time we finish our model, I couldn't care less about what Ben said. That's because Ms. Benedetto hands us each a spoon (reusable, of course!) and announces, "Good job, class! Time to 'take a sample.'"

She pauses and looks at us. Our eyes must be as big as our sugary models. "This means one to two bites only," she says. "You can have the rest at home with your parents."

We take a couple of bites, and I make two conclusions using my skills of deduction. First, I've observed that learning about science can be delicious. Second, I have a hunch that Ben Shaw is up to no good.

Chapter Five

After recess, a few of my classmates share their homework poems. Then Ms. Benedetto assigns our daily quiet reading time. In her class, we're allowed to read whatever we'd like, from nonfiction to graphic novels. We can even reread a book, as long as we're reading. Today I've picked up a new book on oceans called *Ultimate Ocean-pedia*. I'm studying a map of the different zones of the ocean, like the "abyssal zone," when Ms. Benedetto interrupts to make another announcement.

"It's almost the end of the day, and I want to share some information on a new after-school club that I think a few of you might be interested in."

My mind starts racing with the possibilities. If Ms. Benedetto is behind it, it certainly has to be great. Will it be animal-related? Or maybe it's a book club? That would be super fun. Or maybe it is a vegetarian-cooking club? I would consider joining that club, although I'd have a hard time giving up *albóndigas* full-time. Mom's meatballs are just too tasty.

"It's an art club that I'm costarting with the art teacher, Mr. Foster. Would any of you be interested in joining?"

My arm shoots up immediately. I love art! I always participate in the library's art contests. Once, I even placed third with my *James and the Giant Peach* drawing. Not to mention I'm always drawing aquatic creatures in my sketchbook. This club may fit on my dreams list, too. I have to join!

I stretch my arm so far up I feel as if I could touch the ceiling. When I'm excited, it's easy for me to forget that other people are nearby. Ms. Benedetto motions for me to lower my arm some. She counts around the room. Anna, Chris, and a few others have their hands up, too.

"Great! The club will meet after school twice a week, on Tuesdays and Thursdays. Mr. Foster and I have some big ideas on what we could do, too!"

"What ideas?" I blurt out a little too loudly. I turn *roja* and sink down in my seat.

"Well, most of the time, we will just make art. We may draw, paint, mold things out of clay, and learn about artists. We also hope to take a field trip to the Art Institute if we can make it work."

I beam. I've been to the Art Institute in downtown Chicago only once, but it certainly left an impression on me. I especially remember seeing a painting by Georges Seurat called *A Sunday on La Grande Jatte—1884*. From far away, it looks like a completely normal painting. As you walk closer, though, you soon realize that the whole picture is made with little dots of paint. I tried to paint a cute dumbo octopus that way once, but it didn't look as good as Seurat's work.

"But we also have an ultra-top-secret idea." The class murmurs as she continues, "You'll have to come to the first meeting to find out."

I squeal. A mystery!

"Of course, you must get your parents' permission to join," she adds. "It's a big commitment, and we want to make sure you have a way to get home. The last thing we want is for any of you to be stranded here without someone to pick you up."

Ms. Benedetto then posts a sign-up sheet next to the door and hands out permission slips. I make sure to grab one for Mom to sign.

When I get out of school, Nick is waiting outside for me. Because high school starts earlier than my elementary school does, it also ends earlier. That means we can walk home together since Mom is still at work.

"How was school?" I ask him.

"Long," he groans, adjusting his heavy backpack. "And I have a geometry exam this week that I have to study for. At least I have another driving lesson today."

"That's exciting," I reply, trying to sound eager.

While driving sounds a little scary to me, Nick wants to learn so he can eventually be a pizza delivery driver. That's where the big bucks come from, he says. Since he started his lessons, he constantly begs Mom to let him drive. She caved in the first week, and we took him to a parking lot. It didn't go well. Nick kept hitting the brake too hard while Mom sat in the passenger seat, saying *ay dios mío* over and over as he drove around.

"What about you?" he asks.

I tell him all about the science project we made today. Then I tell him the best news. "I am going to sign up for an art club. That is, of course, if Mom says yes." I clasp my hands together, wishing she'll say *sí*.

"Look at you, sis! Sea Musketeers, art club, and swim lessons. You're going to be a jack-of-all-trades." He winks.

I pause for a second, confused.

"That means you have many interests," he explains.

"Oh," I say, not knowing how to respond. I think that was a compliment. It sounds a little like Ms. Benedetto.

"I actually need to find a club to join," Nick continues. "Clubs are the sort of things colleges look for on your application."

My eyes grow big. "But that's four years from now!"

"I know!" he exclaims. "Can you believe that I have to start thinking about college? I'm only two weeks into high school."

The idea of Nick away at college and not at home sounds awful. I want to grab his arm to comfort him, but he usually doesn't like when I hug him, especially in public. Then I remember something important.

"You already belong to one club. Don't forget you're the Sea Musketeers' mentor."

"I could never forget," he says as he messes with my curls. "I live with the president, after all."

Chapter Six

The following Saturday morning, Mom drives me to my weekly Sea Musketeers meeting. She's in a hurry because she's going to the Mexican Independence Day festival for work. The radio station helps put on a big community event to celebrate the day Mexico cried out to receive its independence from Spain. There is even a parade with *folklórico* dancers, floats, and more. It's so much fun. We all used to attend when I was little, but now that Nick is in high school and Mom is the manager, she's only going to stop by for a bit while I'm at my meeting.

As we pull up to Mariel's house, Mom says, "Wish me luck!"

"*Buena suerte*," I reply.

Then I run up to the door and press the doorbell.

Buzz. Buzz.

"*Hola*, Stella," says Mariel as she slowly opens the door to her home.

We usually hold our club meetings at either Mariel's or my house. It depends on whether Mom has to work that weekend or not. Although I like having the meetings at my home, I'm glad when we have them at Mariel's. This way, I don't have to clean my room.

Once the door is open, Mariel strikes a pose. She's showing off her new haircut. She's cut her long hair into a short bob that hits at her chin.

"*Me gusta tu pelo.*" I tell Mariel that I like her haircut.

I tug at my hair for a second. Sometimes I think about straightening it like Mariel's, but I realize I don't have the heart to do it yet. Especially when my family likes to lovingly tousle my curls.

"*¡Gracias!* My new friend, Laura, has the same haircut." She grins widely.

Mariel moved to Chicago from Florida last spring.

During our summer camp, she kept to herself. At first, I thought maybe she didn't like me. Turns out she was just getting used to a new city. Now that she and I are friends, I always try to practice a little Spanish with her since I don't speak Spanish that well. It's a win-win. It makes me happy to practice and her happy to hear it— it reminds her of her friends in Florida. By how much she is smiling, it seems like she is adjusting quite well now to Chicago.

Soon the rest of the group arrives. Since we don't all attend the same school, we usually spend a few minutes catching up. I start to tell Kristen about joining art club. That doesn't last too long because, like always, Logan starts tapping his toe impatiently.

Logan is very practical and keeps the club on track. That is, until he starts chatting about sharks. Then he gets so enthusiastic he won't stop talking about them.

I take his loud tapping as a big hint and say, "Hello, everyone! Let's begin!"

Since I'm club president, I take attendance. I check off everyone's name except for Jenny's in our official roster.

"It looks like Jenny is missing another session today," Kristen notes, crossing her arms.

"She just needs extra time for rehearsing. She's in the advanced dance class now," I reply.

By the looks on their faces, that excuse doesn't go over well with everyone.

Logan's foot is still tapping. I glance over at him. He looks so excited to speak that he might burst.

"Logan, do you have something you'd like to start with?"

I hand him our plush orca. We're a very opinionated group, so whoever is holding the orca gets to speak. It works 60 percent of the time.

Logan cradles the toy orca and begins speaking.

"Now that we're ready, I have big news. Much bigger than an art club."

I turn *roja*. He must have heard me talking to Kristen.

"I'll decide that." Kristen twirls one of her braids and says, "What is it?"

"I finally presented our plastic pledge to my class. And, of course, everyone signed it," Logan announces.

One of the biggest things we did when we started the club was create a plastic pledge. The pledge has easy tips, like carrying groceries in a reusable tote bag instead of plastic bags and avoiding single-use plastics like cutlery. At the beginning of the school year, we all promised to present the pledge to our classes. Presenting it was a breeze, especially for Stanley, Jenny, and me, since we're all in the same class. The whole class wanted to sign it right away, and Ms. Benedetto promised to make our classroom a green space. She set up recycling bins and reminds us not to waste our paper materials. She even keeps extra reusable water bottles on hand in case we forget our own.

Logan continues, "My teacher, Mr. Schuster, was so blown away by the pledge that he had me present it to my principal, Mr. Rana."

"Whoa," says Stanley.

Logan nods. "Then Mr. Rana was even *more* impressed with our pledge, and he wants us to present it at the city council meeting at the end of October."

"Wow," I reply. I'm stunned that Logan was able to share it with his principal. I'm also a little jealous. As president, I should have thought to do that first.

"Wait, what does it mean exactly to present at a city council meeting?" asks Kristen.

"Mr. Rana said that if we do a great job, maybe we could convince them to ban single-use plastic altogether in our school district!"

We leap up and down like a gam of whales. This is huge! The amount of plastic we would save in our entire school district would make a significant difference. Our jumping must be very loud, because Mariel's *abuela* knocks on the door to the room to check on us.

"*¿Qué pasó? ¿Están bien, Mariel?*" She opens the door, asking what is happening and if we're okay.

"*¡Lo siento, Abuela!*" Mariel replies, apologizing. "We just got some great news!"

Mariel then promises we'll keep the noise down, and her *abuela* closes the door, shaking her head but smiling a little.

Kristen excitedly grabs the orca to speak.

"This means we may need to have some extra meetings to prepare. Maybe a couple of times during the week."

Everyone nods, but I secretly gulp. I just signed up for two new activities that meet three times a week.

Thankfully, Stanley says, "Probably not every week. I know most of us have other clubs or activities."

"That's true. I've got chess club," says Logan.

"I just joined soccer," adds Mariel.

"Orchestra." Kristen grins so big you can see her braces. "I'm playing the violin now."

"And I have an astronomy meetup," says Stanley.

I breathe a sigh of relief. I'm not the only one who is busy.

"What should we do to prepare for our presentation?" asks Logan. "It has to be epic!"

I think hard. I want to show the club that Logan isn't the only one who can come up with great ideas for us.

Then it hits me. "We should hold another fundraiser. We can take more pictures of us in action. We can also donate most of the money to an ocean organization and save a little to buy materials for our big presentation."

"Great idea!" says Mariel.

Kristen adds, "Let's brainstorm!"

We spend the rest of the meeting making a list of things we'll need for the fundraiser. We want to have a mix of baked goods, but also some small plastic-free reminders.

As I think about what I can bring, I decide to go big. I want to prove that I'm a dedicated president.

I blurt out, "I'll make two new tote bags with my mom and also a giant poster by next week."

"That's a lot by next Saturday," says Logan. "I can help, if you'd like. Chess club meets only once a week."

"Don't worry; I can do it by myself," I reply. Logan's already done enough by getting us the chance to present to city council. I need to do just as much since I'm the president.

"Oh, okay," he replies softly.

As we continue to divide up tasks, I get a sinking feeling in my stomach. What if I just overpromised? I immediately shake it off. I can whip up a poster, no problem. I'm pretty good at them.

Mom picks me up when the meeting ends. I am about to mention the tote bags when I notice the empty glass food container in the back seat next to me. It's where we put the *quesadilla* for Diego.

"Did you see Diego?" I ask. "More importantly, did he like the *quesadilla*?"

"*Sí*, he actually came to the festival with Izzy," Mom replies.

"How did he know about it?" I ask.

"It's a pretty big event in Chicago. I also mentioned it to Diego the other night, when I bumped into him on our street."

"Oh," I reply. That's strange; she didn't tell me that earlier.

"And *sí*, he loved the *quesadilla*." She grins. "Turns out his family is from El Salvador like your *abuela*. He was very familiar with it. He said it was as good as his mother's."

"Great!" I reply. "I hope I can meet Izzy soon."

"You might be able to meet her next Saturday."

I turn my head to her. "Why?"

"Diego and I are going to get coffee while you're at your Sea Musketeers meeting next Saturday. Maybe afterward you can meet Izzy. That is, if she isn't with her mother."

"Izzy's mom?" I ask. I hadn't considered whether she had a mom and where that mom might be.

"Diego and Izzy's mom share custody of her. They are divorced *como tu papá y yo*."

"Oh . . ." I nod.

Mom and Dad have been divorced for almost five years. Dad lives in Colorado, so I don't see him too much. It doesn't really bother me. He's not a bad person, but he's not a great dad at the same time. Still, I often wish Mom and Dad had a French angelfish sort of relationship. French angelfish rarely travel without each other and stay together for life. Of all the aquatic creatures, they are the most romantic.

"Hopefully, it'll be fun," says Mom. "It might be nice to have a friend in the neighborhood who is also a single parent."

I nod. Mom works super hard and does so much

for Nick and me by herself. I'd be happy for Mom if she had more friends. I can tell that Mom had so much fun at her Girls' Night. Maybe Diego can be her Stanley. Having a friend like Stanley is the best. I'd like that very much.

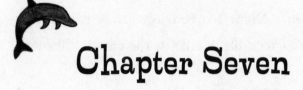

Chapter Seven

"Time for another exciting science project today," announces Ms. Benedetto.

It's Monday morning and the start of a new week. I wonder what sort of project we'll be working on now.

"Is it another project that we can eat?" asks Chris.

Not only does Chris have the loudest voice in the room, but he is also the smallest boy and has by far the biggest appetite.

Ms. Benedetto laughs. "No, not today, Chris."

There are a few groans of disappointment in the classroom.

"Instead, you're going to create a new plant species with your lab partner!"

She writes our project criteria on the board. To complete the project, we must come up with a name for our plant, determine the plant's basic needs, decide where on Earth our plant will live, and draw an illustration of our plant.

"Now, to begin our creation, we must find some inspiration. Grab your creative caps." She motions for us to put our imaginary creative caps on our heads. "Pens, notebooks, and follow me!"

We stand up and march to the library.

I wave at Ms. Morales, our librarian, when we walk in. She has her stuffed goose leaning on the front desk next to the computer. I also notice she has traded the signature purple streaks in her hair for red ones this school year. She comes up to me and tells me, "Stella, we got that book by Sylvia Earle you requested."

She pulls the book from the cart and holds it in front of me. It's a copy of the *National Geographic Atlas of the Ocean*. On the cover is a massive barrel wave, crashing into the sea. I think about how strong the wind must have been to cause a giant wave like that to happen. All I want to do is grab the book and dive in. I begin to open it, but Ms. Morales closes it.

She says, "Don't worry. I'll hold on to it while you work on your research, and you can check it out before your class leaves."

I nod excitedly.

Because we're in the library, we have to whisper. Stanley points at a computer, and I follow him silently. We consult the library catalog and then head over to the nonfiction section.

To begin, Stanley and I find a few books on tropical plants. We both agree that the rain forest has the most colorful plants and, therefore, the best plants for our project.

"Those will be the most fun to draw, too," says Stanley.

We start writing down a list of possible locations.

"Could our plant live in the desert?" I suggest. "Our tropical plant would look awesome there."

"Stella, our plant should live next to or under the sea!" he replies.

I hit my head with my palm. "You're right!" I whisper.

We grab a book on the oceans and pinpoint a few interesting locations, like the Great Blue Hole in Belize and the Skeleton Coast in Africa. Both are dramatic landscapes. The Great Blue Hole is indigo blue and 410 feet deep. The other, the Skeleton Coast, is a sandy desert in Namibia and sits right next to the Atlantic coastline.

Then we brainstorm different types of plants. We don't want it to look like the usual plants you'd see in the ocean, like seaweed or seagrass. That would be less creative. I suddenly remember something I read in one of my ocean books.

"Our plant can't be super deep if it's under water. It needs light to grow. Plus, everything past sixty-five feet looks blue-green because of the limited light."

"Good point," says Stanley.

He pauses and continues, "You know, I can't help but wish our plant could be somewhere in outer space!"

"Maybe there are plants on other planets and we just don't know about them yet," I reply.

"Exactly! And maybe those plants eat humans!" His eyes grow big. "That's why we don't know about them. Anyone who saw one in person was eaten!"

I wince. That sounds scary, but also not very realistic. At least I hope it isn't. He starts to chuckle, which makes me laugh. We have to cover our mouths so we don't make too much noise in the library. I then notice Ben and Jeremy circling around us in the stacks. Ben has his shark grin again, so I know what he is about to say isn't going to be very nice.

"I finally figured out what's going on with you two." Ben looks at Jeremy. "They must *like* like each other."

Jeremy wiggles his eyebrows and nods.

"We're just friends," says Stanley seriously as he closes his book.

"That's what you say," Ben says. "But we're in fourth grade now, and everyone knows boys and girls can't just be friends."

"You're wrong!" I reply in an angry whisper.

"Who made that rule?" says Stanley. "I didn't read it in the class rules."

"That's just the way it is," replies Ben, shrugging. "Everyone knows it."

"My brother told me that, too," chimes in Jeremy.

Stanley and I look at each other with disgust. I can't believe Ben. *Es ridículo.* He's ridiculous. Stanley is one of my closest friends. We've been friends since he moved here last year. Plus, I have other friends who are boys, like Logan in the Sea Musketeers. I certainly don't *like* like him either. Sure, I've thought movie stars and Fabien Cousteau are handsome, but I mostly think we're too young for this kind of stuff. Going out with someone is for older kids like my brother, Nick. I know he has a crush on a girl in his geometry class.

"Ignore him," Stanley tells me. Then he raises his voice a bit to make sure Ben can hear. "He is just bitter that he isn't a part of the fun science group."

Ben scoffs. "Whatever. Don't say I didn't warn you."

I try to ignore what Ben said, but his words stick under my skin like a toxin from a jellyfish sting. I've never been told that I can't be friends with someone. Why should it matter if Stanley is a boy, anyway?

We walk over to another table, but the mood between Stanley and me has shifted. We make zero jokes, and we mostly write in silence. I chew on my pencil eraser. Is it possible that Stanley thinks I *like* like him? I find myself wanting to ask him, but the silence is hard to break. Thankfully, he speaks first.

"Ben is wacky." He takes a breath. "And I don't like you that way."

Whew! I practically drop to the floor.

I reply, "Me either. I don't think I like anyone that way yet."

He nods. "Let's just keep working. He's wrong, and it's only him saying it, anyway."

I nod, but I get the feeling this might be only the beginning. Like a shark, Ben smells blood in the water and isn't going to give up easily.

Chapter Eight

On Tuesday, I try my best to forget about what happened in the library. I have better things to focus on, like my first art club meeting. We gather after school in the art room instead of Ms. Benedetto's classroom. Nick is going to stay at his school doing homework until I'm done with my meeting. That way, he can pick me up and we can walk home together. At the meeting, there are about two dozen of us. Some of the kids are from different grades. While second graders don't intimidate me, a few of the fifth graders do look bigger than me. When I walk into the art room, I am relieved to see Anna and Chris from my class. I pull up a stool next to them.

"Do you two like to draw, too?" I ask them.

Anna shrugs. "I'm a little shy about showing my drawings to people," she says, clinging to her sketch-book. I can relate sometimes. When my drawing is not perfect, I don't want to show anyone else. It took me forever to show Stanley any of my drawings.

"Can I see?" I ask. "I'm sure it's amazing."

She slowly hands me her sketchbook. Chris leans over my shoulder as I flip through the pages. I see swirly drawings of fairies and flowers done in ballpoint pen. It's different from how I draw. I mostly draw sea creatures and portraits, but Anna's drawings are more cartoony. It's very creative.

"I love it," I say.

Chris and I give her a thumbs-up. Anna smiles so hard that her glasses slip down her nose. She has to push them back up.

To jump-start the meeting, we have after-school snacks, like biscotti, cheese wedges, and grape juice.

"We're setting the scene. Imagine we're a Parisian art studio group like the one Monet and Manet had," says Ms. Benedetto. Ms. Benedetto and Mr. Foster even wear matching black berets to go with the theme.

Mr. Foster begins the official meeting. "Thank you for attending our first meeting. In this club, we'll talk about different artists. You will also have extra time to work on individual projects and collaborate on big projects that we'll all work on together."

"To really kick off the new club, we're going big," says Ms. Benedetto. "Think wall-size."

Wall-size? What could she mean? I give Anna and Chris sideway glances.

Chris replies, "I think she means a mural."

"Really?!" I whisper. That would be amazing if it's true. I've never done a mural before, and it would be a new type of art, too. It's also something I can check off my dreams list!

Ms. Benedetto continues, "We have permission from Ms. Morales, our librarian, to paint a mural in the library."

We squeal.

"While we will have time during our club meeting to work on it, it's a big project. We may need to spend a few Saturdays to complete the mural. We'd like to have it done by Halloween."

I gulp. My Sea Musketeers meet on Saturdays. The

president has to be there, but I also really want to paint this mural.

I hesitantly raise my hand. "I have another club meeting on Saturdays. Does that mean I can't be a member?"

Ms. Benedetto replies, "Don't worry. You don't have to stay the whole time. If you need to leave early, that's completely fine."

"The majority of the work will happen during our after-school club meetings," adds Mr. Foster.

Whew. I can still do this, I think to myself.

"But before we get too deep into the planning, let's take a moment to introduce ourselves," says Ms. Benedetto.

I volunteer to go first to get it out of the way. That way, I don't have much time to turn *roja*.

"Hi, I'm Stella Díaz. I'm in fourth grade, and I love marine animals and art."

As the remaining club members stand up to introduce themselves, I can't help but feel distracted about what I just said aloud. I love painting almost as much as the oceans. I've never had to worry about dividing my time between the two until now.

Thankfully, Mr. Foster interrupts my worrying. "Now that we know one another, let's begin brainstorming what our mural should be!"

"Oh, I know . . . superheroes!" exclaims a third grader.

"Yeah, Thor!" suggests a second grader.

Ms. Benedetto chuckles. "That sounds fun, but let's try to think of something that relates to our school."

After we brainstorm for a while, we decide the best idea is to do a painting of our school mascot, the dolphin. I love that idea because I got plenty of practice drawing dolphins for our spelling bee last year.

Mr. Foster says, "Okay, I'd love to see you all come up with a sketch for our next club meeting on Thursday."

"Are you going to choose just one sketch?" asks Chris.

"Good question," Ms. Benedetto says. "It's going to be a real collaboration. Mr. Foster will put together the best parts from all the sketches to finalize our mural sketch. We hope to have the sketch done by next week."

I feel electric. This is all happening so quickly.

Mr. Foster looks at the clock on the wall.

"There is a little time before the meeting ends. So feel free to start drawing right away or chat with your neighbors about ideas."

While Anna and Chris chat, I get to work on a sketch. As I move my colored pencils on the page, I'm excited by the possibility of having my sketch incorporated into the mural. Then I remember the Sea

Musketeers, again. If I explain it's a mural of dolphins, the club should be understanding if I need to skip a meeting. I'm creating firsthand connections to the ocean at my school. I better do a terrific job on my sketch. Maybe I should work on it all night!

When the meeting ends, I zip open my backpack to put my sketch away. I then notice my binder filled with homework assignments.

My mouth drops. I forgot I have to do homework tonight, too. I shake it off and say to myself, "I can do both. I'm a Díaz, after all, right?"

Chapter Nine

The next night, I have my first swim lesson at the YMCA. But before it's time for Jenny and her mom to pick me up, I spend all afternoon working on my mural sketch. I have to catch up because I didn't get to draw as much as I wanted to yesterday. My homework ended up taking so long, and Mom made me stop working at 8:00 P.M. She says she doesn't want me to overextend myself.

Thankfully, my sketch is looking awesome. I drew a pod of dolphins swimming near some waves. I also included a dolphin reading a book because the mural is in the library. I like to imagine that dolphins *can* read since they are so smart and such excellent communicators. They do have their own language of clicks and whistles. I remember summer camp, when I gave the enrichment toy I built to the dolphin. She squeaked when we handed the toy to her, and with her smile and head bob, I knew she loved it. I decide to show the sketch to Pancho for his approval.

"Do you like it?"

He swims around the tank.

"Thank you!" I reply.

When Jenny and her mom pick me up for swim class, I'm a little nervous, but mostly excited. While I do know how to swim, I've always wanted to learn how to do more than just doggy-paddle. I also think it'll be necessary if I ever go scuba diving on undersea explorations.

"Do you know if the class is hard?" I ask Jenny in the car on the way to the YMCA.

Jenny shakes her head. "I'm a little nervous, too, but it should be fun, Stella."

When we arrive at the YMCA, I follow Jenny and her mom into the locker room. I change into my swimsuit. I even have to wear a swim cap and goggles. I look in the mirror at my getup.

It's like I'm straight out of the Esther Williams movies that *mi abuela* likes to watch. In the movies, Esther swims around in a pool with a group of swimmers in these big choreographed productions. *Mi abuela* usually watches those movies with subtitles since she speaks only Spanish. She has visited us in Chicago only a couple of times because she doesn't like to travel as much anymore. Still, it's one of my favorite memories with her. She'd watch them do an aquatic ballet on TV and make me *sopa de fideos*. There is nothing better than her tomato-and-noodle soup. Well, outside of Mom's *albóndigas*.

We rinse off in the shower before we head to the pool. It seems a little silly, but that's to help keep the pool clean from the outdoors. Thankfully, the locker room is right next to the pool. I'm glad I don't have to walk far in a wet swimsuit and squeaky flip-flops.

"Whoa," I say when I see the size of the pool. It's not as large as the ocean, but it's certainly larger than our neighborhood community pool—at least three times the size! It also has much longer lanes to swim laps in. This seems way more serious than when Jenny and I usually go swimming. Since our neighborhood pool is much smaller, we end up just floating around and competing to see who can hold her breath the longest. Those competitions usually end in a tie, although I've been practicing holding my breath the past few days at home. I hope to beat Jenny this time if we're required to do it for class.

"There's our class," says Jenny, pointing to a group

of kids. The class is standing in the pool between the three-foot and four-foot zones. I also see one young teacher wearing a whistle and holding a safety raft. Jenny's mom waits for us on the bleachers.

"Good luck, girls!" she calls out.

"Ready for some megafun?" Jenny pulls her goggles over her eyes and then jumps in.

There is a small splash, and she pops back up to the surface of the water.

"It's refreshing!"

"Is *refreshing* a code word for cold?" I ask, eyeing her. Probably my least favorite feeling is being cold—unless it's the feeling of cold Oberweis ice cream in my mouth.

Jenny shakes her head. "Nope. Sea Musketeers honor. It's warm enough. C'mon in."

"Okay," I reply.

Unlike Jenny, I walk over to the ladder and carefully lower myself into the pool. It feels colder than Jenny said, but when I'm ready, I pinch my nose and finally go under.

When I come back up to the surface, the temperature feels great. And I discover I can stand on my feet in the four-foot area! I was afraid water would go up my nose, but my head pokes out high enough that I can see above the water. It makes me feel grown up.

Our instructor, Megan, checks me off her clipboard and then begins.

"Let's start with a warm-up," says Megan.

We begin class by rotating our shoulders. Megan says this will help warm up our muscles.

"Trust me: You all are young now. When you're older, warm-ups really matter."

Then we jump up and down to loosen up our legs. I look over at Jenny, who is having a blast.

"Stella, it feels like I'm dancing in the water!" she exclaims as she swirls around.

I suddenly realize I'm not sure why Jenny signed up to take classes in the first place. She's already so busy with her dance class that she has missed a couple of Sea Musketeers meetings. How can Jenny juggle one more thing?

"Don't get me wrong. I'm happy you asked me." I take a breath and continue, "But why did you sign up for swim lessons? Isn't dancing your favorite thing to do?"

Jenny replies, "Because it's fun! Plus, my mom

wanted me to try another hobby. One that has no grades and no competition."

I pause. While I do agree that swimming is awesome, I love competition! What's more fun than being the best at something?

Jenny then adds, "Not to mention that I get to spend more time with my best friend."

I smile. I agree with that reason a hundred percent.

After our warm-up, Megan has us practice holding our breath without using our hands to plug up our noses. It's super hard at first. I keep getting water up my nose, but after a little while, I'm able to do it.

Then she passes out kickboards to hold with our hands while we practice swimming across the width of the pool using only our feet. As I kick my feet in the water, I'm reminded of a photograph I saw of a young polar bear learning to swim. Even though they are big, polar bears happen to be graceful swimmers. They can see very well under the water and hold their breath for up to two minutes.

With each leg kick, I feel stronger and more powerful. I'm so glad I signed up for classes, and I guess it doesn't matter that there is no competition. Although if I were to get a ribbon for completing the class, I wouldn't mind that at all.

After a few laps, Megan has us take a break.

One of the kids from our group asks, "When will we use our arms to swim?"

"What you're learning right now is the foundation of swimming," Megan explains. "Once you get the rhythm down, we'll work with our arms next. Before you know it, you'll be able to do this."

Then Megan zips across the pool. She looks almost like a caffeinated frog swimming. On the way back, she is even faster. Almost as fast as Olympian Amanda Beard.

I look at Jenny excitedly. She nods.

"I can't wait to do that!" Jenny says.

After class, when we're back in the locker room, I ask Jenny, "By the way, are you coming to the Sea Musketeers meeting this week?"

"Yup," she replies. "What did I miss last time?"

I tell her all about our presentation for the city council.

"And everyone is bringing a baked good for our next fundraiser . . ."

I stop midway through the sentence. Suddenly I remember that I need to finish two tote bags and a poster for Saturday. With all the excitement of the art club, homework, and swim class, I actually forgot! I begin to panic a little.

Quickly, I ask Jenny, "Do you think you could help me make a poster on Friday after school?"

"I can try," she replies. "It's tough to find time with all the new activities and more homework."

I nod and say, "Who knew fourth grade was going to be so much harder?"

"Could you ask Nick for help? My babysitter helps me sometimes and that makes a difference."

I shake my head. Nick has too much going on to help me, what with his part-time job and homework. "I'll be okay."

When Jenny's mom drives us home, the smell of chlorine lingers on my clothes. My body feels tired, but my mind is wide awake. It's racing, thinking about everything I need to get done for the Sea Musketeers.

Once I get home, I see Mom reclining on the couch. She's already wearing her comfy pj's and watching the news on the Spanish television channel. She looks very tired. I sit down next to her.

"Any good news?" I ask, looking at the television screen. Mom likes to watch the news in *español*. She says you get to see more of what's happening across the world than just in our country. But I can only understand what they are saying half of the time. They speak too quickly for me.

"Not really," she groans. *"Todo está muy mal."*

It must be really bad, because she turns off the television.

"But tell me good news. How was your first swim class?"

"AMAZING!" I reply. I tell her all about class and how much I loved it.

She hugs me. "That's wonderful, *mi amor*. You're turning into your hero Sylvia Earle."

Sylvia Earle is a legend in marine biology and a huge inspiration to me and the rest of the Sea Musketeers. She was the first female chief scientist of the National Oceanic and Atmospheric Administration. She also created these "Hope Spots" around the world to help preserve the ocean. Thinking about her reminds me of Saturday's meeting again. I bring up the fact that I need to make tote bags by Saturday.

Mom looks at me disappointedly. "I wish you had mentioned it earlier. I've had a long day, too."

I frown. Mom does work so hard. I don't want to make her do more work.

I look down and lean against her. "I'm sorry."

I want to tell her that I'm feeling a little overwhelmed by all the things I want to do, but I'm afraid she'll tell me to cut back on something. So I just stay quiet.

Mom puts her arm around me. "It's okay, *mi amor*. Let's work on it *mañana* or Friday. I think we should be able to get at least one done before your meeting. We'll make sure it's *fabuloso*, too. Does that sound good?"

I nod.

"For now, let's go get you a snack and then bother your *hermano*. He's been in his room working on homework."

She grabs my hand, and as I follow Mom into the kitchen, I give her a big hug.

Chapter Ten

Thursday ends up being another busy art club day and Mom has to work late, so we aren't able to work on the tote bags. Instead, Mom and I spend part of our Friday night weekly appointment making them. Mom uses the sewing machine while I select fabrics. We get one whole tote bag finished, and it does turn out pretty *fabuloso*. It has a combination of polka dots and swirly fabrics. It's all in shades of blue, too.

"We'll finish the second one after your meeting," Mom says.

I also finished part of the poster for the Sea Musketeers. I meant to do more, but I got distracted with the final mural sketch, which is due next Tuesday. I actually thought I had finished my mural sketch, but at our last meeting, Mr. Foster pointed out that the pectoral and dorsal fins on my dolphins looked too similar. I can't believe I made such a rookie mistake! I guess I was too excited and rushed a bit. Then Ms. Benedetto suggested that I include more of the ocean environment in the next sketch, so I decided to add colorful coral after I fixed the dolphins. Unfortunately, I lost track of time adding all the details, which meant I spent less time on the poster.

I begin to work on the poster again after we finish the tote bag, but Mom stops me. She insists that Nick and I take a break from work.

"It's our family night, and you two need to have

some fun." She walks over to the closet where we store all the board games.

"You don't have to tell me twice not to work on homework!" Nick says. "Hey, what if I practice driving the car?"

Mom laughs and wags her finger. "No, *señor*. The only *coche* you're going to be driving tonight is the one from Monopoly."

Nick crosses his arms in disappointment.

"Oh, I'll be the dog!" I say.

I love the tiny silver Scottish terrier piece. Saying the word *dog* reminds me of Biscuit. I haven't seen him or Linda in a couple of weeks. I used to see the two of them weekly during the summer, when Linda babysat me.

"Maybe Linda and Biscuit will want to join us," I suggest.

"Good idea!" Mom replies, and picks up the phone.

Linda happily comes over, and the four of us end up playing Monopoly for hours. Biscuit even curls up and falls asleep in my lap for part of the game. He rests his little head on my arm. I try to keep my arm very

still while I play so I don't wake him up. But I don't mind. Having him cuddle with me is the highlight of my day.

When I arrive at the Sea Musketeers meeting the next day, I am filled with dread. I have not completed my poster for the fundraiser, and I only finished one tote bag. I decide to avoid bringing it up as long as I can. Unfortunately, when I get to Mariel's house, it seems like everyone else has their fundraiser goods ready.

Kristen and her older sister updated our blog while Mariel made some "save the oceans" bracelets to sell for our fundraiser. Stanley made stickers that encourage people to use less plastic, and Logan made a huge poster—larger than the one I haven't finished yet.

"What about you, Stella?" asks Kristen. "Where are your tote bags?"

"And the poster?" adds Logan.

"I'm sorry. I don't have everything quite finished," I reply, holding my one tote bag and my half-finished poster. "I ran out of time this week."

I can sense a few glares, especially from Kristen.

"Don't worry about it," Mariel says nicely.

"And I'll help you finish the poster during the meeting," Jenny adds. I look at her kindly. I could hug her right then. I quickly change subjects.

"So does anyone have a good idea for where we can hold our fundraiser?"

Mariel speaks up. "I spoke to my soccer coach about our club. She said we could have our fundraiser at the soccer field next weekend after our game. There will be other games all day, so we'll have plenty of customers."

"Great idea!" Stanley exclaims.

"Maybe instead of the meeting, we could just have

the fundraiser, too," I suggest. "We could discuss the city council presentation while we're selling."

"That's a good idea," says Jenny.

I flash a guilty smile. I'm really only trying to be time-efficient. "When is the game?"

"Saturday afternoon," Mariel replies. She pulls out her soccer schedule, and we all write down the information. Then we do the necessary phone calls home to double-check that our parents will let us go. When they give us the go-ahead, we plan the last details. We all promise to bring a baked good for the fundraiser. Although this time, I don't try to commit to too much. Just chocolate chip cookies from the easy-to-bake section.

After the meeting, Mom picks me up like usual. This time she's sipping on a cup of coffee in the reusable mug she bought after she signed our plastic pledge. I'm surprised she's still drinking coffee, though. She was supposed to get coffee with Diego today during my meeting.

"Did you meet up with Diego?" I ask.

"*Sí.* It was fun! We went to the coffee shop in our neighborhood."

Mmm. They have the best scones and donuts there. We sometimes go in the morning on the weekends.

"And Diego said we could drop by later today if you want to meet Izzy."

"Cool!" I reply. I'm excited about possibly adding a new club member. That will show the group that I'm dedicated and that I'm also an excellent president.

Mom says, "But I don't know how much she'd like to hang out. She's three years older than you. Still, she seemed sweet when I met her at their place."

"Oh," I reply. Mom's been over to Diego's place? I wonder what his apartment looks like.

"Diego is fun. I think we're going to be great friends. Who knows—he might become like my own Stanley." Mom winks at me.

I smile, but then I remember what Ben Shaw said.

Boys and girls past third grade can't be friends. They can only *like* like each other. If that is the case, does that mean Mom and Diego *like* like each other? The evidence is piling up, too. They talk outside secretly on our street. They have had coffee alone together. He even visited her at the Mexican Independence Day festival. My eyes grow big. Mom hasn't dated since she and Dad divorced. I can't imagine her having a boyfriend. Plus, she always says Nick and I are the loves of her life. I shake my head. I'm being *tonta*. It's silly to even wonder about Mom and Diego! They barely know each other. And look at Ms. Benedetto and Mr. Foster. They are grown-ups who are friends, and they're not dating.

"So do you want to meet Izzy now?" Mom asks.

I fake a yawn. "I'll wait. I'm tired."

Even though I don't think that Diego and Mom *like* like each other, I'm not so sure I want to get to know him *or* Izzy better. I'd rather just go home.

"*Sí, mi amor.* By the way, I grabbed one of your favorite scones."

She passes me a paper bag from the front seat. It's a blackberry scone with crystallized sugar on top. When I take a bite, it doesn't taste as good as it normally does.

I smile at Mom to be polite and chew on it silently. I stare out the car window the rest of the way home.

Chapter Eleven

On Monday, as I walk toward my class-room, I spot all the made-up plant-species projects on the walls outside Ms. Benedetto's room. As I look at them, I'm delighted to find that the project Stanley and I worked on has a gold star on it and the word *superb* written on top.

"The entire group was so creative with their plants. I just wanted to show these off to the rest of the school," Ms. Benedetto tells us when she makes her morning announcements.

I feel proud and relieved. Even though I might be a little behind with the Sea Musketeers, at least I'm doing great at school. If only I can get Ben to stop being a pain.

"Class, I hope you're well rested from the weekend. We are now going to start our most exciting and challenging science lab yet."

I gulp. I think I can handle a harder lab. I also do feel well rested because Mom and I watched cartoons at home all yesterday afternoon. I tried to work on homework, but Mom insisted I take a *descanso* whenever a movie was on. Even though we had a fun day together, I sort of wish Mom would have let me get ahead on all my projects, like Nick did before his shift at the pizza shop. I know this is going to be a busy week for me!

Ms. Benedetto says, "We are moving from plants to learning about physics."

She then holds up an egg.

"Anyone want to take a guess?"

I squeeze my eyebrows together and think. All I can think of is *cascarones*. They are eggs that you empty, paint, and then fill with paper confetti. Afterward, you can crack them on someone's head and shower them with confetti. It's messy fun, but I don't think that relates to physics.

"I'll give you a clue," Ms. Benedetto says. "I hope you don't crack under the pressure."

"We're making an omelet?" whispers Stanley. I giggle. At least I'm not the only one who is clueless.

"We're doing an egg drop!" exclaims Ms. Benedetto.

I've only seen an egg drop in movies and on television, but I'm thrilled at the idea of doing it. That's where you make a protective container for an egg and then drop the egg from up high. The goal is to design a container that cushions the egg so well that it doesn't crack when it lands on the ground. I hope we don't break too many eggs in the process. That could get awfully stinky.

"Now grab your partner, and let's get to work." She doesn't give us too many further instructions. She just takes a tablecloth off a big rectangular table and reveals a pile of supplies that we can work with. It makes me happy when I notice that Ms. Benedetto picked mostly reusable materials for our projects.

"Be creative. You'll have a couple of weeks before our big test launch, too."

Ms. Benedetto then puts on Mozart to stimulate our creative juices.

She adds, "And remember, the road to success is paved with failure!"

I wince. I'm not sure about that. I think it's better to get it right the first time. Regardless, Stanley and I get to work quietly. Partially because the room is quiet with Mozart on, but mostly because we are trying to steer clear of Ben. We avoid making eye contact with him. That way, he can't say anything to us. Stanley slips me a note that says, *Beanbags?*

I write back, *Good idea*.

The beanbag chairs are on the complete other side of the room. It's the farthest we can get from Ben. Once we're settled, we start talking in our normal voices.

"Maybe we could put a parachute on the egg," Stanley suggests.

"That would be awfully cute," I say. "But I think we need more than that. The parachute will slow it down, but it still needs something to protect the egg's bottom."

"What if we make it sort of like a hot-air balloon with a little basket?" Stanley replies. "You know, those were the first flying devices before airplanes and rockets."

"Perfect!" I reply. "But let's make it out of only reusable materials."

"Of course," says Stanley.

We then head to the supply table. We grab wooden toothpicks and string to try to make our little egg basket. Then it suddenly occurs to me.

"We should name our future egg. If it has a name, we'll really have to make sure it survives!"

"Penelope!" suggests Stanley.

"I like that," I reply. "But let's keep brainstorming."

From the corner of my eye, I can sense someone staring again. I don't have to look to know who it is. It's the great white shark, the biggest nuisance of our classroom, Ben.

Ben grabs some masking tape and Bubble Wrap from the supply table where we are standing. "Well, look over here, it's Stanley's girlfriend, Stella," Ben says loudly.

I whip my head around, shocked. Now he is calling me Stanley's girlfriend? I mean, technically I'm a girl and I am also his friend, but what Ben is implying is very different. I look around to see if anyone noticed. Thankfully, nobody heard him, at least I hope not.

Ms. Benedetto walks over. "Do you need help with your project, Ben?"

Ben shakes his head and gives Ms. Benedetto an innocent look. As soon as she turns her head, he smirks at me before walking away.

Back by the beanbags, Stanley and I start assembling our toothpicks row by row like Lincoln Logs. We're both silent again.

I'm starting to feel like an egg. Fragile and ready to crack. I think Stanley can tell I'm upset, because he elbows me and says, "I have the perfect name for our egg." He pauses for a moment. "We could name him Humpty after Humpty Dumpty."

"Okay," I reply with a half smile.

Stanley's joke makes me feel better. Despite Ben's behavior, at least Stanley is still exactly the same. But I've got to do something about Ben *rápido*. Because I'm not planning to stop being friends with Stanley anytime soon.

At recess, we get a break from our stuffy classroom, and we practice dropping our basket. We sit on top of the monkey bars with Jenny and Chris, who are egg-drop partners. They ended up together because Anna and Isabel are best friends and naturally paired up. However, I don't think their being on the same team means that Jenny and Chris *like* like each other. At least, I'm pretty sure.

"Good luck, Mr. Basket," Stanley says as I drop it off the edge. Unfortunately, on our first attempt, the basket shatters into pieces. Our egg would have been smashed if it had been in there!

"Maybe the parachute will help slow it down," says Stanley optimistically.

I grab my chin. "True, or maybe we need it to be stronger. Maybe two rows, so it's thicker."

Jenny and Chris launch their contraption next. It's made of balsa wood, but instead of a basket, they made sort of a three-dimensional hexagon. Sadly, it crashes into the ground, too.

I flash Jenny a sympathetic look.

She says, "Thank goodness we didn't have our egg in there."

"Yeah, I'd be sad if little Sebastian died," says Chris.

Stanley and I look at each other. They named their future egg, too. This makes us all burst into laughter. I laugh so hard I can barely catch my breath. Once we calm down, we stare at the wreckage of our projects on the ground below. This project is going to be a lot harder than we thought.

Chapter Twelve

Splash! Splash!

I flutter my legs in the water as fast as I can. It's my second swim lesson, and I have plenty of pent-up frustration. The heavy kicking helps distract me from everything that is stressing me out. Ben is a huge part of it, but most of all, I'm thinking about this coming Saturday.

We made some big progress on our mural at yesterday's art club meeting. Mr. Foster collected all of our sketches, and he is going to present the official final sketch tomorrow. That's also the same day we're going to prime the walls white with paint rollers. I get to wear messy, baggy clothes and get paint all over me. However, I also found out we're starting the mural on Saturday—the same day as our Sea Musketeers fundraiser! Fortunately, our mural session is in the morning, and Mariel's soccer game is in the afternoon. But it's going to be a long day.

So, for now, I just keep kicking with all my might. I kick so hard that I think I could create a tsunami-size wave in the pool. Then I feel a tap on my shoulder. Jenny looks at me.

"Are you okay? You didn't say much in the car ride over here, and you're kicking really hard. I feel like I'm on a boat about to capsize in a storm swimming next to you."

I pause. There is so much I want to say. I really want to tell Jenny about Ben, but part of me thinks that if I tell her Ben is saying stuff about Stanley and me, she'll believe it, too. While Jenny is friends with Stanley, I hang out with Stanley more than she does. I'm also afraid that Stanley and I are the weirdos and that we missed the memo with the rules for fourth grade. Instead, I tell her only part of what's bothering me.

"I'm just a little worried about my new schedule and the egg-drop project."

"Me too," she replies, swirling around in the pool.

"Really?" I ask. Jenny seems so unbothered by everything.

"Well, you saw that our first egg container didn't work, and we don't know what to try next," she says. "And while I love dance class, it keeps getting harder! I'm no longer the best one in the class."

"I doubt that," I reply.

She shakes her head.

"It's true. I'm still very good, but I need to work extra hard. Then with more homework and Sea Musketeers, I just sometimes want a break."

I nod. I feel bad that Jenny is stressed out, but it makes me feel better that I'm not alone. I have been feeling the same way. Just to think, I was so bored at the beginning of last summer not doing anything. How things have changed! I'd love for one day to do absolutely nothing. A day to draw for fun or just wander around the Shedd Aquarium.

I give Jenny a hug in the pool.

She tells me, "Don't worry, Stella. If anyone can do it all, it's you. You make things happen."

I smile. At least Jenny believes in me.

When I get home, Nick looks wiped out. He's lying down on my thinking spot, the rug in the living room. I notice he's still dressed in his work clothes. He must have had a shift at the pizzeria tonight.

"How was work?" I ask, looking down at him.

"Fine." He sits up on his elbows. "Just tiring. I like making pizzas, and my coworkers are awesome, but school is just so much harder this year. It's hard not to get exhausted."

"Same for me, too." Then my stomach rumbles. All the swimming made me hungry. I grab my tummy and look at him.

"Did you bring home any breadsticks this time?"

Nick throws a pillow at me jokingly. "You bet."

As we dip our breadsticks into marinara sauce on the kitchen counter, Nick vents about high school.

"It's just weird. I'm in all the honors classes, which is exciting, but I actually have to work hard for my grades. Before high school, all I had to do was read some, write a paper, and then I got a good grade. Now I have to memorize or do more 'critical thinking.'"

He puts air quotes around "critical thinking."

"And it's crazy because I really care about my grades now. They keep talking about college, and it's so expensive. But if I get good grades, I could maybe get a scholarship, and then Mom wouldn't have to worry so much about paying for it."

He drops his head on the counter. I frown a little. My poor brother has big things to worry about.

"That's a lot, Nick," I say. "Can I help you?"

He looks up at me and smirks. "I'm just venting. I'll be okay, kiddo." He hands me another breadstick. "What about you? What are you so worried about?"

I don't want to bother Nick too much with my personal stuff, especially since he is so busy, so I stick with the smallest issue.

"Have you ever done an egg drop before?" I ask Nick.

"Oh, those are fun! I think we used plastic straws to make ours."

I shake my head. "No plastic straws."

He puts his hand on my shoulder. "I'm sure there has to be an alternative." Then he throws his arms up. "Hey, I've got an idea. Why don't we trade homework? I'll do your egg drop, and you can do my biology homework?"

"If it's marine biology, count me in," I say, kidding.

Nick messes with my curls. "Deal."

I look around. I suddenly realize I haven't seen Mom since I got home an hour ago.

"Where is Mom, by the way?" I ask.

"She texted me while I was at work. She's hanging out with Diego. He wanted to buy a new couch, and she offered to help him pick out one. She should be home soon."

I squeeze my eyebrows together. Sometimes I get frustrated that I don't have a cell phone. I want to check in with Mom and send her fun emojis, but I'm not allowed to have a cell phone until high school. But what bothers me the most is the possibility of Diego and Mom becoming boyfriend and girlfriend. I take this opportunity alone with Nick to ask, "Do you think Mom and Diego *like* like each other?"

Nick laughs. "Whoa, I'm not sure. We haven't really met him yet. It's hard to tell."

"I think it's a little weird," I confess. "Kids at school are saying that boys and girls can't be friends when they get older." I don't point out that it's specifically Ben and Jeremy who are saying it.

"That's not a real rule," he replies.

I feel partially relieved. If Nick says it, it must be true. Then Nick looks at me sincerely.

"The most important thing is, Mom deserves to be happy."

I nod. He's right.

"And if they do start dating, then it's our job to spend time with this Diego and see if he is worth Mom's time. She deserves only the best."

I stare at Nick. It's strange; we're only a month into school, and he seems more mature than ever. He almost seems like an adult.

"When did you get so wise?" I ask Nick.

"Oh, they teach it to you in ninth grade," he replies with a wink.

I think he's joking, but with all his textbooks, I'm not so sure anymore.

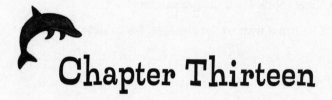

Chapter Thirteen

Today is the big day. The busy day. The day I work on the mural and have my Sea Musketeers fundraiser. I'm ready to take them on. I am as determined as a salmon making its way upstream.

"Remember, you've got to pick me up from my mural at one o'clock on the dot because the fundraiser starts at two," I tell Mom in the morning over breakfast.

"*Stellita*, you didn't tell me about the times," Mom says as she runs her fingers through her hair. "*Mi amor*, I was going to get a haircut. I have a big meeting on Monday, and I need to look my best."

I frown. I think I told Mom last night, but maybe I said it too softly. That sometimes happens.

Mom looks at me and sighs. "It's okay. I'll see if they can switch my appointment to an earlier time."

I feel bad. I never want to ask Mom for too much. That's why I try not to bother her with my homework or projects unless she offers or if it's something she enjoys like baking or sewing.

My mood quickly changes for the better when I throw my painting smock over my clothes. There are already little white specks all over it from when we primed the library wall on Thursday. I'm extra excited to get painting. When Mr. Foster presented the completed sketch for our mural, my drawing of a dolphin reading a book and some of my coral made the final design!

As I'm packing my backpack with the cookies, rolled-up poster, and tote bags for the fundraiser, I hear a knock at the door.

I tilt my head. Is it Diego? I feel a sense of dread. I

still don't want to talk to him right now. Maybe next week.

"Coming," says Mom, walking toward the door.

When Mom opens the door, it's Linda, with Biscuit by her feet. Linda looks a little frantic.

"I'm sorry," Linda says in a rushed voice. "My dog walker is sick, and I'm supposed to meet my grandkids downtown. Do you think you all could take care of Biscuit today? He would only need a walk twice. Once before ten and then a second time in the afternoon."

"Of course!" Mom replies. "We love Biscuit."

Mom turns toward me.

"Do you want to walk Biscuit real quick?"

I look into his brown eyes. He is panting, so he looks like he is smiling. I want to say *Not really* because of everything I have to do today, but I can't say no to that adorable face.

"Of course," I reply.

"Thank you so much, Stella." Linda pulls out ten dollars from her crocheted purse and gives it to me.

"Here, a donation for your fundraiser."

I smile. I'm going to show up to the fundraiser with my completed poster and tote bags, *and* I'll have money to add to our jar right away.

Before we head over to the school, I walk Biscuit around the block. I've walked him once or twice before. This time, he seems to walk especially slow. I think he likes the feeling of walking on the leaves on the ground. He also wants to stop and smell everything on our walk.

"Could you please walk a little faster?" I ask Biscuit politely.

Biscuit looks at me sweetly and then continues to smell the flowers. After a much longer walk than I planned for, we head back inside. I leave Biscuit in the laundry closet with his toys and his puffy bed. Then I rush over to Mom, who is smiling.

"Great news! I moved my appointment up, so *todo está bíen*!"

I breathe a sigh of relief.

"You look very ready for your busy day, *niñita*," says Mom.

I grin tightly and hand her the car keys. I want to tell her to hurry up, but I can't say that to my own mom. Instead, I say, "Yup!"

Thankfully, we arrive at the school parking lot with a minute to spare. Still, I want to make the most of my mural hours. Once Mom stops the car, I open the car door and run toward the school.

"*Espérame, Stellita,*" she yells, telling me to wait for her. "You're going nowhere without me."

I stop and put my hands on my hips.

Mom walks over to me. She puts her hands on my shoulders.

"Stella, I know you're excited, but you need to calm down."

"Okay," I reply reluctantly.

When we walk inside the school, it looks strange. Most of the lights are off except for the hallway lights and the lights in the library. It feels a little mysterious. I like the feeling of being the only ones in the school. I point out my made-up plant species to Mom on the way to the library.

"*Hermosa*," she says, telling me that it looks beautiful.

In the library, the back corner has been transformed into a mini artist studio. Music is playing, and people are talking at full volume. It's very un-library-like behavior! Mr. Foster and Ms. Benedetto are busy arranging paint colors on the table next to piles of brushes. There is even plastic all over the floor and covering the nearby bookcases. I feel all tingly. I can't wait to start the mural.

Mom kisses me on my head.

"I'd tell you to have fun," she says, "but I don't have to worry about that."

I beam.

"See you at one!" she adds.

"On the dot!" I reply. She gives me a thumbs-up as she leaves the library.

Mr. Foster begins, "Okay, my fellow club members, I've transferred the drawing onto the wall. Today we need to block in the big shapes. This is when we are going to apply most of the paint. Don't worry about the details. That comes later."

"We're going to work on the background first," Ms. Benedetto follows. "Who wants to work on the sky or the ocean?"

Of course, I raise my hand to work on the ocean.

Ms. Benedetto gives me a cup of aquamarine paint and points me to my area. "Go get 'em," she says.

I flex my arm and then head to my section. At first, I work on the wrong square of the mural, but thankfully Mr. Foster points it out.

"Sorry, I was just excited," I say as I move over.

When I begin to paint uninterrupted, I forget all

about my stress and worries. With every brushstroke, I get lost in the process. It's almost as if instead of painting I'm swirling in the ocean. I feel like I could paint for hours. They even have to stop me to have a snack break.

As I chomp down on a sunflower butter and jelly sandwich, Mr. Foster walks up to me.

"You've got a real talent for this, Stella."

I grin despite the sandwich in my mouth.

"Do you think you'll want to be an artist one day?" he asks.

I swallow and pause. I never really considered it. I'd already decided I'm going to be a marine biologist, but . . .

"Maybe," I reply, and I'm being honest, too. It feels strange to say that out loud.

We get back to work on the mural, and before I know it, Mom shows up.

"Are you ready to go, Stella?" Mom asks.

"Just a couple of more minutes," I beg. "I only have this last spot to finish. I messed up at the beginning, and I need to finish my square."

Mom looks at me. "Okay, but I don't want you to get upset with me if we're late to your fundraiser."

I look over at the clock. It's only five minutes after one. What could another ten minutes really do?

Mom talks to Ms. Benedetto in the meantime. I just want to finish this one spot. When I put my paint bucket down, I look at the clock again. Oh no! It's one thirty!

"Mom!" I say, running up to her. She's texting on her phone. "We've got to go!"

"*Ay dios mío*," she replies. "I got distracted, too! I was texting with Diego."

I ignore the part about texting because there is no time to think about Diego right now. We're going to be late.

"I'll clean up your brushes," says Ms. Benedetto. "Good luck with your fundraiser."

"Thank you!" I reply. Then Mom grabs my hand, and we run out of the school.

"I checked the directions. It's only twenty minutes away," Mom says as she starts the car. "We should be fine."

Unfortunately, we soon realize that it will take more than twenty minutes. A car accident is blocking traffic on the highway, and we are at a total standstill.

As we sit idly in the car, I watch the clock, hoping that if I wish enough, it will stop. It doesn't. I see it turn one forty-five, then two, and then two thirty.

I slump down in the back seat feeling defeated and angry. If it wasn't for Diego, Mom wouldn't have been texting or distracted and we wouldn't have been late. Why do they *like* like each other?! This marvelous day has turned into a disaster.

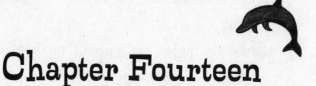

Chapter Fourteen

We don't make it to the soccer field until two forty-five. Our fundraiser is already halfway over!

I spy the Sea Musketeers under a tent on the other side of the field.

I run up to them, panicking and pleading forgiveness.

"I'm sorry! We got stuck in traffic!" I leave out the part about staying too late at the mural. They would definitely not be happy about that.

Mom walks over. "It's true. We were stuck for over an hour."

Mariel's mom says, "That's awful."

Kristen's dad says, "Traffic is the worst."

However, none of my fellow Sea Musketeers say a single thing.

Mom sits by the rest of the parents on the bleachers nearby while I walk over to our table.

I open my backpack. "But I have everything I promised: the cookies, the tote bags, and the poster."

I quickly throw everything down. My poster is extra wrinkly from being in my backpack, and a few of my cookies are crushed. It's not my best work.

Then I grab the ten dollars from my pocket.

"Oh, and I have ten dollars from my neighbor Linda."

I throw it into the cash jar.

Jenny flashes me a kind smile. It makes me feel a little better.

"So what did I miss?" I ask, trying to sound as casual as possible.

Kristen starts, "We've come up with a list of things for the city council meeting."

"My team won the game," Mariel says, wiping a bead of sweat off her forehead. Then she adds, "And we've raised about seventy dollars and had more people sign the pledge online."

"That's great. And now we have eighty dollars. Go team!" I reply, trying to sound like a supportive president.

Logan clears his throat. "And we discussed the club."

"What do you mean?" I ask.

Everyone looks at the ground except for Kristen. She meets my eyes and says, "It seems like you're much busier now, and being the president is a lot of work. I brought up the idea of having a copresident. That way, you could share the responsibility."

Mariel quickly chimes in, "And I nominated Logan because he has great ideas."

My mouth drops. I feel as if someone has punched me in the stomach.

"But I'm handling it," I reply. "And it's not like I have ever missed a meeting before, like Jenny."

Jenny frowns.

I wince. "I'm sorry, Jenny. I didn't mean for it to sound bad. I know you love your dance class. I just mean I'm always here."

Jenny gives me a half smile, but I can still tell I hurt her feelings some.

Mariel puts her hand on my shoulder. "We just want to make it easier for you. The city council meeting is a big deal, and we want to do the best job we can."

I shake my head. I'm not willing to hear it. I only messed up this one time, and it's not really my fault. And the other time, when I didn't finish the tote bags, is not a big deal. I still got them done before the fundraiser.

Kristen nods. "We all voted on the idea of making Logan copresident, and we agreed we'd like to try it."

"This is wrong." My voice gets louder. "You wouldn't have this club without me. I came up with the idea in the first place."

Stanley walks over to me. "It's okay, Stella. Nobody is kicking you out. It's just sharing the load."

"It's true. Plus, I only have my chess club," says Logan. "I just have more time to help. We will be a great team."

I cross my arms. This is royally unfair. I want

to make a big scene, but I get quiet instead. We're still doing our fundraiser, after all. We sell a few items before the end, including my tote bags. One of the soccer moms pays twenty dollars for the two totes.

"I love it," she says. "Such a clever design!"

I mutter, "And I'm the one who came up with the idea for the tote bags, too."

"What did you say, Stella?" asks Kristen. Her face looks like she's trying to be nice.

I shake my head. I am not ready to talk to these traitors yet.

A few Sea Musketeers try talking to me some more, but I continue to ignore them.

Instead, I plot how I'm going to start a new club without them. Then at three thirty on the dot, I leave silently with Mom.

Chapter Fifteen

On the car ride home, my anger turns into sadness. Mom keeps looking at me in the rearview mirror.

"*¿Estás bien, Stella?*" she asks as she parks in front of the house.

"Yeah," I reply, but I feel my lip quivering.

Mom says in a soft voice, "I don't believe you, *mi amor*. I could tell you had an argument with your group."

She turns around so I have to look at her face-to-face.

"You can tell me."

Suddenly I burst into full tears. I confess that I'm feeling overwhelmed and how, worst of all, the Sea Musketeers want Logan to be copresident.

"And I feel like . . . ," I say in between sobs, "I'm getting everything wrong!"

Mom reaches behind and grabs my hand.

"*Mi estrella*, you're doing great. I'm proud of you for trying to do new things. I also really don't think your club members are trying to do something *malo* to you."

"It *feels* very mean," I reply, pouting.

"The club is a big responsibility. During the summer, it's easier to focus on only your club, but during the school year, when it's busier, it makes sense to share more of the workload."

I nod. Deep down I know she's being sensible, but

it doesn't feel like that. It feels like they are stealing my idea from me.

She hands me a tissue to wipe away my tears. I have to go through a few tissues to clean up all the waterworks.

"Come, let's get out of this car and grab Biscuit. We need to take him on a walk."

Biscuit showers me with kisses when we open the laundry-closet door. It's like he knew I needed some comfort.

As we walk him around the block, Mom says, "I think that we all need a little break."

"More movies?" I ask. I'd be happy to curl up on the couch with a blanket again.

Mom replies, "That's always nice, but we also all need to unplug and relax. I'm thinking a getaway."

"Where?" I ask.

"Well, Diego has invited all of us to go camping at Indiana Dunes National Park next weekend. That's what he and I were texting about earlier. He's been planning to go with Izzy for a while. He says there is space at his campsite for us to go with them."

"Camping? Don't you remember last time?"

Mom laughs. "*Yo sé*, but we went in November last time in Wisconsin. That was a very bad idea. It's still early October, and it feels great outside."

I nod. That's true. I'm wearing only a light sweater today, not a parka and long johns.

"But we don't know what we're doing," I say.

I also think back to my own personal camping adventure last month. Jenny and I freaked out, and it was only in our backyard. I can't imagine camping in the wilderness, where there are sure to be large predators nearby. How will we survive?

"Diego goes camping all the time," Mom replies. "This also isn't going to be rugged camping. He texted me the site, and I checked it out online. There are plenty of people nearby, regular bathrooms, showers, and everything. It would be only one night, too."

I look down at Biscuit. He's lying on the grass, blissfully soaking up the outdoors. He looks happy. I want to be that happy. I guess the outdoors could be good for me. I've also been avoiding the Mom-and-Diego situation for a couple of weeks now. This camping trip would give me a good opportunity to see firsthand what is really going on. I also think it would be a nice excuse to skip a Sea Musketeers meeting for one week. I'm not ready to see any of their faces yet.

I look up at Mom.

"Okay, let's do it."

"Great!" says Mom. "Nick already agreed. I'll call Diego and let him know."

I pick up Biscuit, and we head back home.

I'm still uneasy about the camping idea and Diego, but when Biscuit snuggles up against me, I instantly feel better.

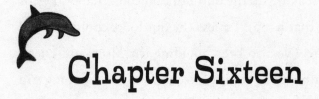

Chapter Sixteen

The next week at school I keep to myself a little more. It's not that I am truly upset with Stanley or Jenny, but speaking to them reminds me of what happened at the fundraiser. And I still feel a little hurt. The Sea Musketeers are just such a part of who I am. They're like my gills—without them, I can't breathe. This change feels like I might be losing a part of me.

It takes me a few days to even mention the club to Jenny, but I sort of have to. I finally talk to her about the Sea Musketeers during swim class.

"I'm really sorry again for calling you out at the

fundraiser. I'm a lousy BFF," I say, looking down at the water.

"No, you're not," Jenny replies as she playfully splashes me.

I splash back.

She then says, "Just don't do it again, bestie."

"Promise."

I feel relieved. Thank goodness Jenny understands. I couldn't take it if she was upset with me, too.

I then ask, "Jenny, can you tell everyone I can't go to the meeting this week? That I have a family camping trip?"

She swirls around me. "Are you sure you don't want to tell them? Everyone feels bad. No one meant for you to feel that upset."

I shrug. "I just need a break for a week."

"Okay, Stella," she replies with a little frown.

The remainder of the week isn't all bad in Ms. Benedetto's class. Stanley and I don't chat much while working on the egg-drop project, so Ben mostly leaves us alone. The highlight of the week is painting the mural at art club on Thursday afternoon. That's when all my problems and everything else evaporate, at least for a little bit.

Finally, Saturday comes, and it's time for our camping trip. We're all dressed for the part, too: puffy vests and plaid shirts.

"This is as midwestern as I'll ever look," jokes Mom. It's true. Mom often wears a *rebozo* around town. That's a large Mexican scarf. Mom says she likes to carry a little bit of Mexico with her everywhere she goes.

When Diego knocks on our front door, Nick greets him. Diego shakes his hand.

"It's nice to finally meet you, Nick. Are you ready to go camping, *señor*?"

Nick sort of smirks. "I think so."

Diego looks over at our gear and takes out his checklist. He puts a pencil mark next to every box on his list.

"It looks like the Díaz family is prepared." Then he

turns to his daughter. She's been standing behind him quietly. She has curly hair like me, but she is taller and wears glasses.

"I'm sorry, *mija*. You still haven't met everyone. This is my darling daughter, Izzy." He adds, "The apple of my eye."

Izzy rolls her eyes and says, "*Papi*." The way she does it, you can tell she actually doesn't really mind it too much.

"Nice to meet you, Izzy," I reply.

"What grade are you in, Stella?" she asks in a friendly tone.

I tell her I'm in fourth grade, and she tells me she's in sixth grade.

"Fourth grade was one of my favorite years in elementary school," she says with a genuine smile.

I smile back. I think Izzy might be as nice as I hoped. Maybe she and I can start our own save-the-oceans organization. I have a few names for the new club in mind already.

"Well, we are all packed up in our car, Perla," says Diego. "Do you want help loading up your car?"

"Thank you, but I think we've got it, Diego," Mom replies.

Diego gives us all high fives. "Then Izzy and I will hit the road. See you all there!"

As we pack up the car with our tent, sleeping bags, and a cooler full of food, I ask Mom about a few last items to pack.

"Can I bring the tablet?"

"Nope!" she replies, moving things around in the trunk to make room for more gear.

"Homework?" I ask.

"No-no," she replies in a singsongy voice.

"Then what can I bring?" I ask, frustrated.

Mom stops to think.

"A book, your sketchbook, and playing cards. That's it. The idea is to take a *descanso* and clear your mind."

I feel a mixture of relief and stress. While I'm excited about doing nothing, I also worry about falling behind. I should be working on my egg-drop device. We are doing the big launch on Monday, and we've only had failure after failure.

"Don't worry about homework," Mom says, sensing what I'm feeling. "You'll have Sunday afternoon to work on it."

After we load up the car, we head for Indiana Dunes National Park. We soon leave the Chicago skyline behind, and the buildings get smaller as we drive. Before we know it, the landscape is much emptier.

"There's nothing out here," I say, looking out the window.

"Isn't it great?!" says Mom. "We're only an hour and a half away from home, too!"

I suddenly regret agreeing to this trip. What if I get bored? I wonder how long it would take me to walk home.

When we arrive at the visitor center of the national park, we meet back up with Diego and Izzy. Diego has already picked up our campsite packet.

"Hey, Díaz family. Do you want to see something fun?" He pulls out a navy-blue booklet from the back pocket of his jeans.

"It's one of my prized possessions." He flips to the front. "This is a national parks passport book."

"What's that for?" asks Mom.

He excitedly explains, "At every national park, monument, or site you go to, you can get a cancellation stamp in this book. I'm about to go get mine for Indiana Dunes. Want to come along?"

My eyes grow big. I love stamps, stickers, buttons, you name it. We follow him over to the kiosk, and he stamps his booklet. Then he flips through the pages and points out some of his favorite stamps.

"This one is from the Gateway Arch in St. Louis. That was really cool. You can go up the arch, too, in this small pod elevator and everything."

"It looked futuristic, like *Star Trek*," adds Izzy.

I notice a stamp of a horse in the booklet. It has a big *X* on top of the horse's face.

"What's that one?" I say, pointing.

Diego starts chuckling. "That is from Assateague Island National Seashore. My friend and I tried to go camping there once, but we got chased away by wild horses! They stole our food and everything."

My mouth drops. Horses are so cute! I can't imagine them being bullies like that. I study Diego a little bit. The passport book is pretty interesting.

"You can look at this more later. *¡Vámonos!* Our adventure awaits," says Diego.

As we follow Diego in his car to our campsite, I'm blown away by the size and shapes of the sand dunes. Not only are they big, but they also look so clean and smooth, like clouds. I want to roll around on them like I do in the snow. With all the sand and how empty the skyline is, it almost looks as if we're at the ocean instead of Lake Michigan. I could stare at the scenery for hours. It's beautiful.

Unfortunately, our campsite is not on the dunes.

It's in the middle of the woods nearby. It looks like an average park and definitely less adventurous. We begin to unpack.

"Do you all know how to set up your tent?" asks Diego.

"Oh, we're experts," Nick jokes. He gently elbows me in the side.

We set up the tent a few feet from Diego and Izzy's tent.

When we're done, I sit down at the picnic table at our site. I begin feeling antsy. It's strange not to be doing something. I should be at my Sea Musketeers meeting now or painting the mural. Not to mention doing homework. I'm starting to regret this trip again. I decide to pull out my sketchbook to entertain myself when suddenly I feel a bite on my hand.

"Ouch!"

I look down at the source, and there is a mosquito! I quickly flick it away.

Diego looks over.

"I thought it would be too late in the year for them."
Diego frowns. "Better use the bug repellent."

He tosses me a can of natural repellent, which I quickly spray on. Before I know it, I'm engulfed in a cloud of sticky, orange-smelling mist.

Diego adds, "Watch out! That stuff can be a little strong. Just use a little bit at a time."

Too late, I think as I cough. Worst of all, my hand still feels itchy.

I scratch my hand and look over at Mom and Diego. I'm observing carefully for any clue or hint that they *like* like each other. I haven't seen any hand holding, hugs, or—ew—kisses, yet. I'm staring at them like a hawk until I hear Diego say to Mom, "Don't forget to keep the food in the car or in the food locker."

"Why?" I ask, interrupting their conversation.

Diego turns toward me. "Well, there aren't any bears out here. Those haven't been seen in the park in several years. But there are other critters, and the smell of food will attract them to our site. We should really have the food out only when we're preparing a meal or eating."

My eyes grow big. Critters? What type of critters? Will they try to eat me? Are there snakes? A mountain lion? Or worse, wolves? This was the worst idea! I'm bored, I'm itchy, and I might not make it out alive.

Chapter Seventeen

After our campsite is set up, Mom sug-
gests we hike over to the dunes. I'm happy to have
something to do because I was having a hard time just
sitting there. It seemed like everyone was working on
something. Mom was inflating our sleeping pads, Izzy
was helping her dad with their tent, Nick was gather-
ing firewood, and I had nothing. No one wanted my
help, so I tried drawing, but I felt too restless. Drawing
reminded me of Sea Musketeers posters and homework. The exact things I *didn't* want to be thinking
about.

We grab the map and begin the hike. I'm looking
everywhere for potential predators. Soon Diego begins

to identify different birds along the path with his bin-oculars. The first bird he points out is black with a fiery red spot near its wing.

"That's a red-winged blackbird. They usually live by water and marshes."

He pauses, and his eyes light up again. "And do you hear that? It's a woodpecker. Let's try to find him."

I think Diego must love birds as much as I love marine animals.

We stop and scan the trees. I can't see anything but trees. Then Izzy spots him. "It's over there, Dad!"

"Good eye, Izzy!" exclaims Diego.

Izzy beams, and Diego gives her a side hug. Look-ing at the two of them, I am jealous for a second. I wish I had that kind of relationship with my dad. Diego seems like a really good dad. A reliable dad.

"How come you know so much about birds and the outdoors?" Mom asks Diego.

"I joined the Boy Scouts when I was ten. We had

just moved to the United States from El Salvador. Those kids were my first group of real friends." He peeks through his binoculars. "And I guess I never grew out of playing outdoors."

Diego's experience with the Boy Scouts kind of sounds like me and the Sea Musketeers. Before them, I really had only Jenny and Stanley for friends. I miss my club mates for a second, but I quickly ignore the feeling. I'm still too upset.

We soon arrive at the dunes and stand there, taking in the epic view. I just want to run on top of them and roll around.

Then Diego takes a runner's stance.

"What are we waiting for? Let's have some fun!" Diego says as he takes off.

We bolt toward the dunes. It's exhausting to climb all the way to the top, but once we do, we walk around. It's the most fun I've had in weeks. Tumbling on the dunes, I even forget about the Sea Musketeers, the egg drop, and Ben. After making a sand angel, I look over at Mom. I notice she's sitting on a dune staring at the lake by herself.

Wiped out, I walk over to Mom and plop down beside her.

"*Es mágico*," Mom says in a soft voice.

I nod. It is magical. The water shimmers like gold in front of our eyes. I feel at peace. I also feel brave enough to ask Mom about Diego.

"Mom . . . do you and Diego *like* like each other?"

Mom laughs. "Are you asking if we're dating?"

I nod.

She looks at me. "No, we're not." She pauses. "I think he's great, and maybe someday there might be something else, but our friendship is still very new."

"Oh," I reply, letting out a sigh of relief. "But why aren't you dating?"

"We both have kids, and you guys mean the world to us. I'd rather take my time to make sure that's something worth doing. Right now, it's just great to have a new friend nearby."

"Well, I don't think it would be bad if you dated Diego," I say, giving her my approval. "He's nice."

"*Gracias, Stellita*," she replies. "And if anything were to change, you and Nick would be the first to know. *Te prometo*."

We stay at the dunes until sunset. Then we head back to our campsite for dinner. Mom and Diego prepare our food on the grill, while we kids sit around a campfire. I thought I would be terribly bored just looking at a fire, but I get sucked in watching the flames.

When dinner is ready, we move to the picnic table. Izzy sits down next to me. It's the closest I've been to her all day. Even on our hike, she mostly stuck by her dad's side while I stayed near Nick and Mom. Maybe she'd like to chat! She has a book in her hand, but she's not reading and she's sitting pretty close. I could even ask her about forming a new oceans club with me. I have two possible club names, but they are not particularly great.

I struggle with how to begin. I think about using a conversation starter. I have a good one, too. Like, did you know the ocean contains more historical artifacts than all the museums in the world combined? While that fact is incredible, I decide against using it. Instead, I ask a simple question.

"Why did you like fourth grade the most, Izzy?"

Izzy puts down her book. "I had the best teacher that year, Ms. Christie. She told everyone that she was one hundred and eight years old. I also had class with my best friend that year. Oh, and the egg drop, of course!"

I sigh. "I'm working on an egg drop right now. We're doing terrible!"

Izzy flashes a sympathetic look. "I know it's hard. We made so many mistakes until we made it work. It felt great when we did."

"I don't know if we'll figure out a way to make it work," I say, frowning.

"I can give you some pointers if you'd like," she says. "I wouldn't have been able to make my egg drop work without some help."

"Really?" I reply.

Izzy says, "Totally! I was stuck until my dad stepped in. We found videos online that gave us ideas."

I rest my forehead on my palm. That's so smart. Why didn't I think to do that?

Izzy nods knowingly. "I'd be happy to share my experiences." She pushes up her glasses. "You want to do that right now?"

"Yes, please!" I exclaim.

I run and grab my sketchbook.

Izzy begins, "The most important thing about the egg drop is that you use different materials to help support the egg. You can't rely on only one material to protect it. It's sort of like a team carrying the load."

I pause. That's just what Stanley said about having a copresident for the Sea Musketeers. Maybe Stanley is right about the club.

Izzy and I continue to chat over dinner about the project and what it's like in sixth grade.

Izzy says, "I have to admit, middle school is a little scary, but I'm lucky I have most of my classes with Eli."

"Who is Eli?" I ask.

"My best friend," Izzy replies.

My mouth drops. "Your best friend is a boy?"

She laughs. "*Yeah*, and he's awesome." Izzy then says, "And some people have teased us, but whatever. Those aren't people I'd want to be friends with, anyway."

I smile. Izzy has a point. I'm starting to realize that Ben is just immature.

I'm chomping down on a hot dog when Izzy notices some of my Sea Musketeers drawings in my sketchbook. I was working on a logo for the club a few weeks ago before everything turned upside down.

"What's that?" she asks.

"Oh, it's for a club I'm part of. It's called the Sea Musketeers."

She replies, "That's cool! You're so lucky to have a club."

I nod silently. She looks like she wants to chat more about it, but thankfully Diego asks, "Do you guys want any s'mores?"

"*¿Qué es eso?*" asks Mom.

Nick replies, "Oh, I've had s'mores ice cream, but never a campfire one. It's a marshmallow-and-chocolate thing."

"Don't forget about the graham cracker!" says Izzy.

Diego prepares our first campfire s'mores. Mom thinks they're too sweet, but I think the ooey, gooey, melty treat is perfect. I make a second and third one by myself. We then put out the fire and stare at the night sky. In the complete darkness, I can see more stars than I've ever seen before. They even twinkle, like the lullaby. I understand more why Stanley is obsessed with outer space. I almost have the same feeling looking at the sky as I do when I stare at the ocean. Altogether, I have to say this evening has been a great adventure.

Then, with a belly full of hot dogs and s'mores, I fall fast asleep in the tent in between Nick and Mom.

Chapter Eighteen

In the morning, we wake up extra early to see the sun rise over the lake. Although we spent the night in our sleeping bags on top of thin pads, I feel it's the best sleep I've had in days. I stretch my arms wide above my head. Maybe this whole camping thing really was just what I needed.

"I can't even remember the last time I saw a sunrise," says Nick, sleepily sitting on the dunes. Nick might not be a morning person, but he made an effort today to see the early-morning light show. It is well worth it, too.

After breakfast, we head back so Nick and I can get started on our homework. I can still smell the campfire on my clothes on the car ride home. I like it. It reminds me of sitting by the cozy fire. I stare out the window. I think I can see the Shedd Aquarium on the horizon. Then I start thinking about the Sea Musketeers. While I'm still hurt about the whole thing, I sort of understand why they suggested we should have a copresident. I was sort of lying to myself about the little mistakes I was making. It is also a lot to be the president, and it makes sense to share the load.

I am still staring at the Chicago skyline when Mom brings up how overwhelmed I've been. It's almost as if she could read my mind.

"Now, I don't want you to give up any of your activities," Mom says.

I sigh. "Whew."

Then she continues, "But . . . I think we need to come up with a new schedule. Times in the week for you to work on extracurricular activities and homework.

That way, we can make sure you're getting everything done and not feeling overwhelmed. We should also write down every project you're working on so we don't lose track of anything."

"Yes, please!"

"And we can't forget to include fun in this schedule. When you don't take breathers from work, it's easy to get upset and burned out." Mom makes eye contact with me in the rearview mirror while she talks. I turn *roja*.

Mom adds, "Like no working during our Friday night appointments. I set that up in my own schedule a long time ago so I could always make sure we'd have fun together every week."

"*That's* why you call it our weekly appointment?!" I ask. I hadn't even considered that Mom made us part of her schedule. I just assumed Mom came up with a funny name for our Friday nights. Like the way she calls our feet *patas* instead of *pies*. That's because she thinks it's cuter to call our feet ducks' feet than regular plain feet.

"Of course! I wasn't born a superwoman. I had to learn," Mom replies, looking at me in the rearview mirror with a smile.

Nick groans a little.

Mom pokes at him. "And you two are my super*bebés*."

He scoffs, but I can see his secret smirk as he replies, "Okay, Mom."

We work on my schedule once we get home. Mom uses a chalkboard in the kitchen to write down what we decide I should work on each day. This way, I can see it in big clear letters while I'm working. She even blocks in break times in pink chalk.

"Now it looks extra fun," Mom says.

When we're done, I know I need to do two big things today. I have to work on the egg drop, which is on my official schedule, but I also have on my personal list to talk to the Sea Musketeers. I start with Stanley. I give him a call, and he comes over to my house to work on the egg-drop project.

"Did you like your camping trip?" asks Stanley in an extra-polite voice. I can tell he is still being careful around me, like he has ever since the Sea Musketeers fiasco.

"It was AMAZING!"

Then I ramble on for ten minutes about the trip, until I spy the chalkboard and remember it's egg-drop time.

I tell Stanley, "But the best part is, Izzy also has done the egg-drop project. She had some pointers for us."

"Awesome! Like what?" he asks.

I get so excited that I ramble off all her suggestions at once. "Izzy recommended we think about protecting Humpty from all angles because we don't know which way it will land. She also suggested using empty toilet paper rolls because they are light, using a few different materials to protect the egg more strongly, and, oh, watching online videos for inspiration."

"That's helpful! My dad recommended watching videos, too!" Stanley then looks around. "Do you have any toilet paper rolls?"

I nod and dump a box full of them onto the table.

"I got them from our recycling, Linda's, and Diego's."

"Awesome," says Stanley. He then opens up his backpack. "I also brought this old, broken umbrella for our project."

I stare at the misshapen umbrella. Is it supposed to rain tomorrow?

Then Stanley adds, "I thought we could use this for the parachute, since my dad was going to throw it away."

"Ohhh! Genius!" I reply.

Stanley gives me a high five. "Go team Humpty!" he cheers.

Mom brings over the laptop, and we watch a few videos online. After a little while, I finally work up the courage to ask Stanley about yesterday's Sea Musketeers meeting.

"How did it go?" I ask, trying to be as cool as a sea cucumber.

"Good," he says. "But everyone feels awful and missed you. Still, Logan did a good job. I think you two would really make great copresidents."

I look at Stanley. He's always honest with me. Logan also has great ideas and is so enthusiastic about the club. Without Logan, we would get sidetracked too much at our meetings. We also wouldn't be presenting our pledge to the city council. Plus, all the names I came up with for my possible new save-the-oceans club were *no bueno*. The Ocean Angels and the Sea Mermaids just don't have the same ring as the Sea Musketeers.

I take a breath. "Okay, I'll give it a try."

"Really?" says Stanley. "I think that's great!"

"But we're hosting the next meeting at my house, and I'm calling everyone to let them know. I need it to be on my terms."

"Sure, whatever you need, partner," says Stanley.

Then I remember one more thing.

"And tomorrow we're dealing with Ben head-on," I say in my most determined voice.

"Deal. This whole ignoring him thing is not working," Stanley replies.

Then Stanley and I do a fist bump and continue with our egg-drop planning.

Chapter Nineteen

The next morning, I walk toward the entrance of the school with the determination of a crab that won't give up. While it feels cooler outside and I have to wear a jacket and scarf, I feel fiery hot inside.

Last night Stanley and I were able to launch an egg from a ladder in my backyard, and it didn't break. I called everyone about Saturday's Sea Musketeers meeting, too. They all agreed to come to my house for the next meeting. With that handled, I feel like I can manage everything today. I'm confident that we're going to ace this project and that we're going to deal with Ben the bully once and for all.

Unfortunately, I don't get to take on Ben right away. I am prepared to, too. I have my game face on. I feel like a *luchadora* ready to pounce in the wrestling

ring. Instead, once the bell rings, Ms. Benedetto has us put our jackets back on. Then she takes us to the top of the school for our egg drop. We are wasting no time before getting started.

Other than a wall around the edge of the roof and some boxy equipment, there isn't much to look at. But still, we feel very special to be standing on top of the school.

"I didn't even know we could get up here!" Jenny shouts.

"This is only for special occasions and, of course, with teacher supervision," replies Ms. Benedetto, her teeth chattering a little. She adds softly, "I guess the cold front came in early."

We huddle beside Ms. Benedetto against the wall, staying close together so she can keep an eye on us, but more for the warmth. We look over the edge. While we're only one story off the ground, it still looks awfully far down to the pavement below. I can also see Mr. Don, our custodian, bundled up on the ground waving up at us. We wave back.

"Why is Mr. Don out there?" asks Chris.

"This might be a little messy, and we don't want to leave raw eggs on the ground," Ms. Benedetto explains. "Plus, he's going to give us the thumbs-up if it worked or not."

Then she hands each team an egg from the egg carton, and we insert them into our devices.

It's the perfect amount. One dozen eggs for one dozen teams, I think to myself.

Then I look over the edge again. From this height, I start to have doubts about our dear Humpty's well-being.

"Who wants to go first?" Ms. Benedetto asks, rubbing her hands together to stay warm.

Before I can say anything, Stanley says, "Stella and I will go first."

I gulp. I guess it's time. I hold our egg holder made out of toilet paper rolls over the edge while Stanley prepares the parachute.

"Okay, on my count," he says. "One . . . two . . . three."

I let go.

I can barely look as our egg falls to the ground. I cover part of my eyes.

"Did he survive?" I ask Stanley.

Ms. Benedetto looks down at Mr. Don. After what seems like forever, she gets the thumbs-up from Mr. Don. Humpty survived!

"Hooray!" we exclaim, and then we give each other a big hug.

"*Ooooh* . . . Stanley hugged his girlfriend!" exclaims Ben.

He starts making kissing noises with his mouth. He's being so loud the whole class can hear him. It's hard not to when we're all so close together.

I look around to see how everyone else is reacting, but Jeremy is the only one snickering. The rest of the group looks confused or annoyed.

"Ben Shaw, stop that immediately. I will not tolerate that kind of distracting and mean behavior in my classroom," says Ms. Benedetto. She says it in such a stern voice that everyone in the class is taken aback.

Ben's face gets white.

I take the opportunity to say something.

"Ben keeps saying that Stanley and I *like* like each other," I say, looking at Ms. Benedetto. "But that's not true; we're just friends."

"Is that so?" Ms. Benedetto asks Ben.

Ben looks at the ground and doesn't respond.

"Well, class. Let me clear this up for you. We are no longer in the Victorian era, or even the twentieth century. It's the twenty-first century, and girls and boys at any age can be friends."

She continues, "And you and I, Ben, are going to have a chat about this later."

I feel relieved. It's over for now. I also realize that Stanley and I should have just brought it up to Ms. Benedetto earlier. Sometimes a problem is too big to handle on your own.

"Now let's keep going. It's freezing!" says Ms. Benedetto.

Chapter Twenty

The next day after school, I go to my art club. I'm in great spirits, too, because I found out that Stanley and I received an A on our egg-drop project. I can't wait to tell Izzy about it. Ms. Benedetto also changed the class seating arrangements at the end of the day so each table would have new tablemates.

"I was planning on doing this at the end of the six weeks, anyway," Ms. Benedetto tells the class. "Who cares if it's a couple of days early?"

Jenny and Chris are now with Stanley and me at our table, while Ben is separated from Jeremy. Ben is now sitting at a table full of girls. I hope he learns to make friends with girls or it's going to be a long six weeks for him.

While we're working on the mural, Chris comes over to talk to me. He looks a little serious.

"I'm sorry Ben was picking on you and Stanley. I don't know what happened to him. He just sort of became mean over the summer. That's why I stopped being friends with him."

I feel bad for Chris. It feels awful when you grow apart from a friend or have an argument.

"It's hard to lose a friend," I say. "I hope he goes back to being like his old self."

I mean it, too. Even if Ben is not my favorite person right now, I don't want Chris to be lonely. I would rather see Ben be nice and Chris have his friend back.

Chris looks a little sad as he shrugs his shoulders.

I add, "In the meantime, I'll be happy to be your friend."

"Sure," he replies with a grin. "I have absolutely no problem being friends with girls."

We get back to painting. I smile the whole time I work. Part of it is that my day has been great so far, but it's also because I'm painting the part of the mural where the dolphin is reading a book.

At the end of the club meeting, I walk up to Ms. Benedetto. I have one final thing I need to talk to her about, and that's Saturdays. I feel nervous about it, but I blurt it out.

"I know I missed last Saturday's painting session, but I can't always come to Saturday club meetings. I have my Sea Musketeers meetings at the same time. That's my save-the-oceans club I started with my friends. I hope you're not upset with me."

"Stella, that's not the case at all. I think it's great that you have many interests. You're still so young. It's important for you to discover what you like and what you're passionate about. I'd never make you choose between the two."

"Really?" I smile with my whole face.

"Definitely. Come whenever you can."

As I leave the school with Nick, I feel warm inside. Outside, though, it feels colder than the day before. We're both bundled in our parkas now.

"It's like we skipped fall and jumped straight into winter," Nick says while putting gloves on his hands.

Out of the corner of my eye, I notice a pair of adults

holding hands leaving the school. Because of the big coats, I'm not sure who it is, until I spy leopard-print boots. Then I realize that it's Mr. Foster and Ms. Benedetto! I turn *roja* a little bit. Out of all the people I suspected, I guess two people do really *like* like each other. I laugh.

"Dating is weird," I say to Nick.

"Ain't that the truth. I've got one week to ask Erika to the homecoming dance." Nick sighs. "I should just ask her tonight. I'm supposed to text her anyway and go over geometry homework together."

"She helps you with geometry? But you're so smart," I ask, stunned.

Nick chuckles. "I know." He messes with my curls. "But sometimes it's smarter to ask for help, too."

"Oh," I reply. I wish I had realized this earlier.

Then he stops. "But why do you say dating is weird?" He looks at me suspiciously.

"No reason," I reply, and keep my mouth shut the rest of the way home.

Chapter Twenty-One

On Saturday morning, the three of us are sitting in the kitchen eating breakfast together. Nick is up early, already getting a head start on homework while he chomps down on his cereal. He looks extra happy this morning. Erika must have texted back and said yes to homecoming.

"*Niños*, they are calling for snow tonight," Mom says as she looks at her phone.

"What?" I drop my spoon in my cereal. "It's not even Halloween yet!"

"You know the weather in Chicago, *mi amor*." She continues, "*¡Está loco!*"

"Does that mean we won't have school on Monday?"

asks Nick excitedly as he closes his American history book.

"I think we'd have to get a lot of snow for that to happen, but you never know," says Mom.

Nick groans and reopens his textbook.

Mom then says, "Oh, Stella. By the way, Linda called and asked if you could walk Biscuit this morning."

I bite my lip. As much as I'd like to walk Biscuit in one of his adorable sweaters, it might be too much with everything I have to do this morning.

I hesitantly reply, "I probably shouldn't. I have my meeting today, but maybe tomorrow? That is, if everything isn't covered in snow."

Mom looks pleased. "*Sí, amor*. That sounds like a good decision. I'll let Linda know. I'm sure she can ask someone else to do it."

I stand up proudly. "Well, I better get ready for my Sea Musketeers meeting."

"*¡Es la verdad!*" says Mom. "I've got Bagel Bites, too."

I pause to think. "Only bring them out if it's going well."

"Got it, *jefa*," she replies, saluting me.

I go upstairs to clean. Mom always insists that I have a clean bedroom and bathroom for the meetings.

While I put things away, I get nervous about the meeting. The more I think about the fundraiser, the more I realize I was the one acting badly by throwing a fit. It wasn't Logan or any of my fellow Sea Musketeers. All they wanted to do was help. I hope the meeting goes well. At this point, I think my life would be ruined if I can't make it work with the Sea Musketeers anymore.

Stanley and Jenny show up at the house early before the meeting to lend moral support.

"It's going to be fine," says Jenny. "And don't forget what I said in swim class."

I reply with a smile, "I've got this."

It makes me feel better, but I still nibble nervously on one of the pretzels that Mom put out as a snack for the meeting.

Finally, the rest of the crew shows up on time.

Unlike our usual meetings, no one is really catching up about the week. It's sort of eerily silent, like the deep sea.

"Should I take attendance?" asks Logan, breaking the silence.

I look over at him.

"Or you could do it, Stella," says Mariel.

I take a deep breath. It's about sharing responsibility. *I don't have to be in charge of everything,* I say to myself.

"You can do it, Logan," I say sincerely.

Logan takes attendance and then says, "Does anyone want to start talking first?"

He glances at me. I pick up the toy orca.

"I've given it a lot of thought, and it's a good idea to have a copresident."

I can see everyone loosen up.

I continue, "The city council presentation is a big deal, and I have a busier schedule now. The club is one of the most important things to me." Then I say the hardest part of all. "And I'm sorry I reacted badly at the fundraiser."

I look at the ground. I feel a little teary-eyed just saying it aloud.

No one says anything at first. Then like a giant wave, everyone surrounds me and gives me a big hug.

"Don't worry," says Mariel. "We're just glad you're okay!"

"We wouldn't have this club without you," replies Kristen, hugging me extra hard.

I nod with a smile. I guess everyone was right. I feel foolish for even thinking they were trying to steal the club from me. Now that I think about it, the Sea Musketeers is like the egg-drop project. Each of us has to work together to succeed. If one person tries to bear all the weight, they will break. Sort of like me. I turn toward Logan.

"Do you want to keep running the meeting, co-president? You're doing a great job."

Logan grabs the toy orca excitedly.

"Okay, I want to discuss the city council meeting. It's only two weeks to go, and we need something big to impress them."

"A bigger poster?" asks Mariel.

We shake our heads. We all stare around trying to brainstorm a good idea.

I rest my chin on my hand. Then I come up with something. "What if we ask Mr. Kyle and Ms. Susan to come be our special experts?"

"Our Shedd Aquarium camp leaders?" says Mariel, standing up.

"OMG, that's so smart! No one could deny experts!" exclaims Jenny.

I nod.

"They also said we could contact them whenever we want," says Logan.

"Let's email them now," Kristen says excitedly.

"I'll ask my mom," I say.

I run downstairs to talk to Mom. She's reading a book on the national parks that she picked up from the library.

"There are so many amazing places to visit!" she exclaims. Then she looks at me and asks, "Is everything okay?"

I nod. "Can we use the computer to send an email?"

"Of course, *Stellita*," she replies. "I'll grab the laptop."

"And can we have Bagel Bites now?" I say with a smile.

She claps her hands together. "*Mi amor*, I'm glad it's going well! I knew it would."

Then we walk up the stairs with the laptop and the warm Bagel Bites in hand.

Chapter Twenty-Two

I wake up the next morning feeling extra cozy in my bed. When I think about stepping out of the blankets, I quickly change my mind. I can already tell my room is cold. Wintry cold.

"*Levántate*, Stella," says Mom, telling me to get up out of bed.

"Why?" I reply, sitting up.

She heads to my window and opens the curtains. "It snowed!"

I look out the window to see the first snowfall of the season. It's more than a *poquito*. It's a couple of feet, and it's still snowing! It's always funny when it snows in the fall. The oak tree in our backyard still has many of its colorful autumn leaves, but they are all blanketed in snow. I also know many of those leaves will fall off by the end of the day with the weight of the snow.

"Do you think we'll miss school tomorrow?" I ask Mom excitedly.

"It looks like you might!"

Mom and I then grab our snow boots and parkas and head outside to the backyard to enjoy the wintry weather. After our fill of snow angels, we decide to head back indoors.

"You know what I'd love to do now?" says Mom.

"What?" I ask eagerly. Mom has the best ideas.

She laughs. "Daytime camping!"

"What? Don't you remember our camping trip in Wisconsin?"

"Indoors, I mean!" she replies, laughing even harder.

"Yes! Can we invite Diego and Izzy?" I ask. I hope to finally ask Izzy to join the Sea Musketeers now that everything is back to normal with the club.

"Great idea!" she replies, and then gets on the phone.

Nick wakes up after he hears us moving the living room furniture around.

"What are you two doing down there?" He has his blanket around him. "And why is it so cold?"

"It's snowing, Nick!" I reply.

"Big deal, it always snows in Chicago," he says. Then he looks out the window. "Whoa! That's a lot of snow for October."

I giggle out of excitement. Mom and I nod.

"I guess no driving lessons today," he says, scratching his head.

"Instead, we're going to do indoor day camping, *niño*!" says Mom.

I add, "And Diego and Izzy are joining us in a little bit."

Nick doesn't say anything. He just drops his blanket and helps us make space for all the sleeping bags. In Nick code, that means he's in, too. We then start a fire in the fireplace. Finally, we use the largest pot we have to make Abuelita, Mexican hot chocolate, on the stove. It's better than regular hot chocolate because it has spices in it. At least, my family thinks so.

As soon as we're all set up, Diego and Izzy make the hike across the street with their sleeping bags.

"I can't believe we're camping again so soon, Díaz family," says Diego as he enters the house.

The five of us spread our sleeping bags on the living room floor. Mom even puts on an online video of a fireplace.

"That way, we're extra toasty," she says. "With two campfires."

We sit around playing board games as the snow continues to fall outside. I don't know whether we will have school tomorrow or whether the Sea Musketeers will persuade the city council to ban single-use plastic. I also don't know if my new schedule will work as perfectly as I hope. But none of that matters for now. I'll have plenty of time to worry about all my big dreams later. All that matters is, in this moment, everything around me on this snowy day is *perfecto* and I wouldn't change a single thing.

Author's Note

When imagining a third story for Stella, I thought there is no bigger adventure than starting a new grade. A new grade brings opportunities and challenges, both of which Stella is now better equipped to handle.

I hope Stella's story encourages all kids to dream big as well. The kids who might be shy. The kids who take speech classes. The kids who emigrated from a different place. I see myself and Stella in you. And just like Stella, you are all stars and full of potential.

Childhood is the time to dream big, when anything is possible. Kids should stay curious and explore their different interests. People often ask me whether I always knew I wanted to make books for children when I grew up. The truth is, I didn't. I considered being an architect, a director, a lawyer, or a *jefa* like my mom. Having so many interests and curiosities informed my point of view and my books. That said, it's important to take breaks just as Stella's mom encourages her to do. Some of your best ideas come when your mind is resting. Dear reader, don't be afraid to ask for help when things get overwhelming, too.

Finally, on a different note, I wanted to share why I chose to use italics for the Spanish words in my books about Stella. This was a thoughtful decision to make the language clear and to make the story inclusive for all readers, especially ones who are Stella's age or younger who may not be familiar with Spanish or may have trouble speaking it. I know firsthand how challenging it can be when you feel confused between the two languages. My hope is that all readers feel welcome to get to know Stella and join her adventures.

Acknowledgments

I'm thrilled to be writing acknowledgments for a third time. First, I have to thank my family: my mom, my big brother Alejandro, his family, and my extended family in Mexico. I love you all. Big thanks to my friends, especially Mary Benedetto for being my beta reader. I also must thank my boyfriend, Kyle, and our rescue dog, Petunia. Thank you for making my life sweeter and supplying endless amounts of love. I'd be lost without you.

I'd also like to thank the people involved in the creation of this book. Thank you to my agent, Linda Pratt, and my great editorial team, Connie Hsu and Megan Abbate. Connie and Megan, you push me every time, and I'm a better author because of you. A huge thank-you to Kristie Radwilowicz for her wonderful collaboration on the covers. She's the wizard behind the fantastic text design and composition. Thank you to everyone at Roaring Brook Press, including Jennifer Besser, Beth Clark, Michelle Gengaro, and Avia Perez. I have to also thank the marketing and publicity teams at Macmillan, especially Lucy Del Priore, Katie Halata, Melissa Croce, and Mary Van Akin. Thank you for championing this book and getting it into the hands of educators and librarians. You are the best!

Finally, I'd like to thank the readers who made the series possible. These are the educators, students, SCBWI, and the bloggers. I have to especially thank Pernille Ripp and the Global Read Aloud community. Having the opportunity to share *Stella Díaz Has Something to Say* with readers around the world was life changing. The experience made the world feel a little smaller and a little brighter. It's also an experience I will never forget. Thank you!

Help Stella save the ocean!

1. Carry a Reusable Bottle

2. Say No to Plastic Straws

3. Carry a Tote Bag and Say no to Plastic Bags

4. Say No to Plastic Cutlery

Visit StellaDíazBooks.com
to take the pledge.

Stella is determined to make this year her best one yet— but after life takes unexpected turns, Stella will have to fight to keep her perfect year on track. Not to worry, because Stella Díaz is to the rescue! Right?

Keep reading for an excerpt.

Chapter One

"Do you have the grapes?" I shout excitedly from the living room.

My big brother, Nick, joins in. "Yeah, Mom. It's almost midnight."

Mom pokes her head in from the kitchen.

"Si, niños. Un momento."

Our neighbor Izzy looks up from her phone. "Grapes?" She's here with her dad, Diego, to celebrate with us.

"Grapes are one of our New Year's traditions," I explain as I smooth out my sparkly sweater.

Izzy nods, but she still looks puzzled as Nick fills her in on our yearly grape tradition.

Mom says it started in Spain, but now people all over Latin America do it. Each person gets twelve grapes, representing the months of the year. You're supposed to make a wish with every grape you eat. However, Nick and I have never paid attention to that. We believe whoever finishes all twelve grapes first must be the luckiest. Unfortunately, Nick always wins. It's probably because I giggle too much at Nick to eat quickly. He looks like a chipmunk with his cheeks filled with grapes!

But I've been hoping that this year will be different. I have my game face on.

I love that New Year's Eve feels different from every other day of the year. It's the one night we get to stay awake past midnight and wear fancy clothes just to sit at home. More than anything, I love having the chance to start over and the opportunity to make the next year even better than the last. It feels magical!

It's also awfully nice to have friends with us for this New Year's. Even Biscuit, Linda's Chihuahua, is here, and he is wearing his nicest sweater. Linda is in the

Bahamas with her family, and we're dog sitting until she gets back tomorrow. I think having Biscuit here is a sign there might be a dog in my future.

"Look, the ball is dropping!" exclaims Izzy, pointing at the television. On the screen, the announcer is counting down in Times Square.

We count along from ten to one. Then at the stroke of midnight, Mom and Diego blow their party horns.

Nick and I race to eat our grapes as Izzy slowly nibbles on hers while texting her friends. Nick looks like he is going to beat me when suddenly he gets distracted by his phone buzzing. This is my chance to win! When I finish my last grape, I open my mouth and stick out my tongue.

"All done! It's official. I am the luckiest!"

Chapter Two

I sleep in later than usual the next morn-ing, and so does Biscuit. Not Mom, though. When I go downstairs to the kitchen, she's dressed in her exercise clothes and is busy setting up the blender. I watch as she tosses in some yogurt, milk, blueberries, and frozen spinach.

"*¡Buenos días! ¡Feliz año nuevo!*" she exclaims, wishing me a happy New Year.

Mom looks at the spice rack and grabs the cinnamon.

"It's time to eat well and start our resolutions."

Before winter break, we learned about resolutions

in Ms. Benedetto's class. They are basically goals people make for the year.

"And what are your resolutions this year, Mom?"

Mom turns on the blender and shouts over the motor's whirling noises.

"Focus on my wellness and get a promotion at work." She taps her chin. "Oh, and for us to become US citizens, of course."

I get all tingly inside when she says the word *citizens*. Mom is two days away from taking the big citizenship test. It's a hard test you take when you are trying to become a United States citizen. You have to know the answers to a hundred questions about US history, even if they ask only ten of them. I've been helping Mom by pretending we're on a quiz show and I'm the host asking her the questions. If Mom passes, then she, Nick, and I will finally become citizens and have a special ceremony.

"What about you, Stella? Do you have any resolutions?"

I nod. *So many*, I think. I grab my journal from my backpack to show her.

Besides getting a dog and becoming citizens, one of my resolutions is to have the Sea Musketeers pledge finally approved by our school district. Last fall, we prepared to do a big presentation for the city council so they would approve our pledge to cut back on plastic, but at the last minute, it was canceled! However, we finally

have luck on our side. We received our letter in the mail with the new date in March.

"Those are some good goals, *mi amor*!" Mom says, kissing my head. Then she grabs her thick green smoothie and pours herself a glass. "Yum, *que delicioso*!"

She fills up a second smaller glass and sticks a metal straw inside. "Do you want to try?"

I look at her eager expression. It's hard to say no to Mom, so I take a gulp.

Even though the smoothie is muddy green like seaweed, it's surprisingly tasty! I give her a thumbs-up.

Mom's cell phone buzzes and lights up. She leans over and takes a peek at the screen.

"Linda messaged. She's back home."

I stare down at Biscuit. "Time to go, my little friend."

We walk outside, and I ring Linda's doorbell. She must be excited to see him, because she opens the door right away.

"My two favorite creatures! Come on in!"

She motions us to follow her inside. She smells of coconut-scented sunscreen and has tan lines on her face from her glasses.

Linda picks up Biscuit. He covers her face with sloppy kisses.

"I missed you, too," she says, giggling. Then she turns to me. "How did my boy do?"

"He was perfect." I clasp my hands together. "Guess what! Mom says we might be able to get a dog this year, too."

"I'll put a good word in for you with her." Linda grabs something from her purse. "Now, this is for taking care of Biscuit," she says as she hands me a few bills.

Linda gives me some money whenever I take care of Biscuit, although I never keep it. It always goes directly into the Sea Musketeers club.

She continues, "And this is a little gift from my trip."

I squeal when she hands me a small cardboard box. When I open it, there is a little sea turtle carved out of white limestone resting on top of cotton balls.

"I saw it and immediately thought of you. The gal who sold it at the store also said it would bring good luck."

I give Linda a big hug. "Thank you!"

Then I wave goodbye and head back home. As I squeeze the sea turtle in my hand, I think, *This is just what I need for my perfect year*.

Chapter Three

I wake up energized even though it is as dark as the abyssal zone outside. Winter makes the days shorter, and usually all I want to do is sleep in, but today is special. It's the first day back to school after three weeks, and more importantly, it's Mom's citizenship-test day. We all get up extra early, including Nick, to help Mom review during breakfast.

In between bites of my warm cinnamon-flavored oatmeal, I grab a couple of the homemade flash cards.

"Oh, here are two questions combined into one," I say, reading a card. "Who was the first president and the father of our country?"

Mom replies, "George Washington. *Eso es muy fácil.* Ask me a harder one."

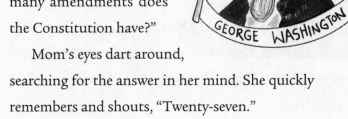

Nick sips his chocolate milk and then asks, "How many amendments does the Constitution have?"

Mom's eyes dart around, searching for the answer in her mind. She quickly remembers and shouts, "Twenty-seven."

Nick flashes her a thumbs-up. "Remember you only have to answer ten questions. Not all one hundred of them. It won't be that bad."

Mom shakes her head. "That's true, but I don't know which ten they will ask from the list. We better do some more."

Mom nibbles on her toast. She promises she'll celebrate with a full breakfast afterward. For now, it's only dry *pan tostado.*

While Nick asks her another question, I suddenly

have the worst thought. It's something I hadn't considered until this very moment. It might be the reason why Mom is so concerned about passing the test. I burst and say it aloud without thinking.

"Mom, if you fail the test, does that mean we have to move back to Mexico?"

While I love Mexico, I haven't lived there since I was two years old. That would be an ocean-size change, not to mention I'd have to leave the Sea Musketeers and all my friends.

Mom leans over to give me a kiss on the head.

"*No te preocupes*. It just means I'd have to take the test again, and I'd prefer not to do that."

I let out a huge sigh of relief and lean over the counter dramatically, which makes both Nick and Mom laugh.

Mom looks up at the clock. "It's time to go to school, *niño*."

"Don't worry, Mom. You're going to ace this test," says Nick as he stands up, grabbing his backpack.

We hear a car horn beep outside. Nick's best friend,

Jason, and his mom are here to drive Nick to school. As he walks toward the front door, he shouts, "Good luck, Mom."

"*Gracias, niñito.*"

After Nick leaves, I finish getting ready for school. Mom drops me off a little early so she can have extra time to get to the immigration office.

As I open the car door to get out, I look back at Mom. She is sitting still and staring ahead like she's concentrating really hard. I instantly recognize what she's feeling because I have felt it often. She is nervous! Seeing Mom anxious is probably the oddest thing I've ever seen in my life. Well, maybe the oddest thing outside of a picture of a fangtooth fish. It's a deep-ocean fish with a mighty underbite. Anyway, Mom is the bravest person I know in the world. She's the one who encourages me to try new things and to have courage. Still, we've been working toward our citizenship since we moved to the United States seven years ago. Now I'm almost nine and three-quarters. That's a long time!

I struggle to find the perfect thing to say to her, and then I remember my good-luck charm. I dig into my pencil bag.

"Do you want to borrow my sea turtle?" I ask. "Linda says it's lucky."

"No, that's okay, *mi Stellita*. A hug from you is all the luck I need."

"Then I'll squeeze you extra, *extra* hard."

Mom gets out of the car, and I throw both arms around her. I squeeze so hard that I even groan as I do it. That makes Mom belly laugh.

"That works. *¡Ahora tengo mucha suerte!*"

After I say goodbye, I head toward my school. Down the main hallway, I spy Mr. Don, our custodian, cleaning a water fountain. Even though I don't speak to him too often, I decide to be more outgoing and say hi. I take a deep breath and make sure to project my voice so he can hear me. That's a trick I learned in my old speech classes with Ms. Thompson.

"Good morning, Mr. Don."

He steps back, looking a little startled. I turn *roja* like my red sneakers. I must have projected too much.

"Hello, Stella!" His kind expression puts me at ease. "Did you have a good break?" Mr. Don is the best at remembering students' names.

"I did, and guess what!" I say, practically ready to burst.

He tosses a paper towel into a trash can and smiles. "What?"

"My mom, brother, and me might become citizens soon!"

He throws his arms up in the air. "Congrats! That's amazing, Stella."

I knew Mr. Don would be excited for me. He was born in the Philippines and became a citizen when I was in third grade. The whole school threw him a surprise assembly to celebrate. We even had cake! He looked so happy, with tears of joy in his eyes. I hope it's a life-changing experience for me, too. I'm about to ask him how it feels to be a citizen when the first bell rings.

"Uh-oh. You know what that sound means. Time to head off to class, missy."

I nod. "Have a good day, Mr. Don."

I walk into my classroom and see Anna, Isabel, and Jenny at my table. I run over to my seat and look around the room for Stanley. I make eye contact with

Ben Shaw, but he glances away. Although he doesn't pick on me anymore since Ms. Benedetto chatted with him about it, we don't exactly talk much. When the last bell rings, I scan the room one more time.

"Where's Stanley?" I whisper to Jenny. "He should be here. He was supposed to get back yesterday from Texas."

Jenny shrugs her shoulders. "I haven't seen him."

Not having Stanley in class is a little disappointing, but I can't focus on that, because Ms. Benedetto begins speaking. "Good morning, class. I trust you all had a great break."

Everyone chatters excitedly to each other. A few students even shout aloud what they did over the break.

"I went ice fishing," shouts Jeremy.

"I ate so many cookies," chimes in Isabel.

Ms. Benedetto holds her right arm in the air and raises her left hand to her mouth to signal to us to quiet down. "I thought we'd ease into our first day back with a video."

The class roars happily like a colony of sea lions.

As Ms. Benedetto finds the video online, Jenny says

softly to me, "You won't believe what I heard. My dance company is going to participate in a regional competition. I could win a ribbon and graduate to the next level at my school!"

"That's amazing," I whisper. "I can help. You can borrow my lucky sea turtle that Linda just gave me for the competition. You will definitely win."

"Yes, please!" she says, beaming.

While the video plays, I notice the good-citizenship bulletin board beside me. I should study it carefully since I'll be a citizen soon. At least I really hope so. I quietly read each of the star-shaped messages on the board. I see words like *honesty*, *kindness*, and *community*. The word repeated the most is *help*. It seems like helping others is the biggest part of being a good citizen. If I make this one of my resolutions, then it might send some *buena suerte* to Mom during her test. I'm determined to do whatever it takes. Because if Mom fails the test today, we'll remain aliens for longer.

In third grade, I discovered that since we're not citizens, we are called "aliens" by some. It means we were born somewhere else, but for a while, I kept imagining scary space aliens. Thankfully, Nick taught me that aliens are cool. For instance, many important people who contributed achievements to the United States, like Albert Einstein, were also aliens. While I almost like the word now, it doesn't quite have the same ring as *citizen*.

The clock moves as slow as a sea anemone, but as soon as it strikes three, I race out of the building with my lucky sea turtle in hand. Since Mom took a personal day from work, she should be out here. I search frantically for Mom and Nick until I find them standing by a wintry-looking tree. They both look serious.

"Oh no! You didn't pass!" I throw my arms dramatically into the air.

Nick starts chuckling.

Mom smiles. "I passed! And I got all ten questions right!"

I jump up and down. It's hard to stretch my arms up all the way with my parka on, but I try my best.

Mom says, "And can you believe I had to write a sentence down to prove that I can speak English?"

I stop jumping and roll my eyes. My mom has been speaking English since she was my age. She began taking classes in elementary school back in Mexico.

"When are we going to have our ceremony?" Nick asks.

"They said in about two months," Mom replies. "We'll get a letter in the mail with all the information soon."

I squeal. I wish it were tomorrow, but that is not too far away. Really, what's two months in what is going to be my best year ever?

"Well, what do we do now?" Nick says.

I reply, "I know. First, we get Oberweis ice cream."

"I hope they have the Berry American flavor!" Mom claps her hands.

Meanwhile, I tuck my lucky sea turtle back into my pencil bag. I know for sure it somehow helped my mom! My new resolution to become the most helpful citizen also must have been lucky. Now I just have to live up to my promise.

Join Stella Díaz on all of her adventures!